About the Author

Abbie Morley currently lives in Nottingham, England with her poodle, Mr Pudding, and spends most of her time riding and looking after her two ponies. Abbie has had a lifetime love of reading and writing novels, having a keen interest, in all things history related, even attending an archaeology dig on a castle in the name of research for her new book, *The Gods of Belware.*

The Gods of Belware

Abbie Morley

The Gods of Belware

Olympia Publishers
London

www.olympiapublishers.com
OLYMPIA PAPERBACK EDITION

A CIP catalogue record for this title is
available from the British Library.

ISBN: 978-1-80074-341-0

This is a work of fiction.
Names, characters, places and incidents originate from the writer's
imagination. Any resemblance to actual persons, living or dead, is
purely coincidental.

First Published in 2022

Olympia Publishers
Tallis House
2 Tallis Street
London
EC4Y 0AB

Printed in Great Britain

Dedication

I dedicate this book to my dear friend, Judy.

Acknowledgements

Firstly, I would like to thank my dear friend, Judy, who helped in many stages of the process from reading early drafts to helping with cover ideas. Secondly, I would like to thank my partner, Thomas, for putting up with my countless shenanigans and encouraging me in my writing. And lastly, I would like to thank all my family and friends for supporting me through this journey.

Chapter One

People say she is half god half devil, people whisper these rumours, these rumours turn into legends. These legends get passed from generation to generation. But in fact, if people knew the truth, that she was just an ordinary girl, with an extraordinary story, legends wouldn't be born.

Her birth name was Charlie; she came from a lower-class family who didn't seem to have two pennies to rub together. However, she could no longer bring herself to use that name, she resented her family and she was glad she would never see them again; they had made sure of that. She was a new person now so therefore a new name was needed; she went by the name Kit.

Kit was one of six children born to Martha and Jedson Conway. They lived in a small dusty shanty town in a misshapen hut. The scenery was bare and barren, nothing grew, nothing prospered.

Being the eldest, they had picked her to send away. They said it was for the good of the family, they made a point of saying she was saving the family from starvation. At first, she was more than happy to go to the far-off land they called Retega, but once there, escape was her only thought.

Her parents had sent her to Retega research laboratory in the year 2050 when she was only fourteen. Retega was renowned for their scientific research into military war weapons, their new ambition was to create super humans. God-like creatures with super strength or modifications to their bodies decreasing the need for weapons. Most of the experiments lead to death of the victim but a few survived. Kit was one of them, whilst at the laboratory she had met a girl called Daisy. Her family had also sold her for the money. The two became inseparable and would talk through the cell walls about what they would do once they had got out.

The day they escaped was a blur in Kit's memory, it had all happened so quickly. She could remember running through endless sterilised corridors, reaching dead end after dead end. It had been Daisy's idea to enter the restricted access area stating that they had no choice at that point in time. Kit could remember the bright lights, the shiny wheels, and flashing buttons. She remembered the bewilderment she felt, the confusion written across Daisy's face, the slamming of fists on the locked door. The panic rose in both of them as they started pressing buttons, pulling switches. Then there was pure silence that's what Kit remembers the most, the purest of silence and the sheer bright light that pierced through them.

"Kit are you even listening to me?" Daisy said with folded arms.

"Yes, sorry my mind was miles away," she replied with a small shake of her head.

Daisy sighed. "Well, I was saying how I can't believe this is our last duty as soldiers and we're having to take the princess to see Prince Geoffrey," Daisy moaned.

Kit laughed back at her. "Yes, no epic battle to end our careers I'm afraid."

To be honest Kit didn't mind it this way, she was tired of fighting for the king and his endless crusades. They seemed pointless to her, gaining more land but not looking after the people. More and more people were entering poverty as taxes kept rising to keep the crusades going. The state of the kingdom was a constant worry for Kit, and the princess Nekite marrying Prince Geoffrey from the neighbouring kingdom Carak probably wasn't going to help.

The princess was sat in the palace gardens surrounded by neatly cut grass and her five ladies in waiting, doing cross stitch and giggling away. Kit and Daisy were the princess's guards; this meant they had to protect her from any danger that may come her way. They had been assigned her guards now for two years. This didn't stop them being called up for major battles, however, as they were the ones, they called half gods half devils. They hadn't been defeated yet, but the king only liked to bring them out in big battles mostly to scare off the opposition. Throughout all kingdoms it was a well-known fact of the power that lived within these palace walls. Surrounding kingdoms were scared of the god-like creatures thus stopping any invasion, which was another reason for the king to keep Kit and Daisy within the palace. Servants didn't dare look at them, never speaking to them, just scurrying around them. They too, feared the rumours they had heard. Kit had tried to engage them in conversation. It would be nice for her to have more than just one friend in this place, it just hadn't happened.

The princess's wedding was to take place in two weeks and preparations were well under way; banners were going up the best silverware being polished and the wedding dress having pure gems sewn into an intricate pattern. It was said to be the wedding of the century, combining two kingdoms for both the wealth and security. Kit thought Prince Geoffrey of Carak was not to be trusted with his long shoulder-length blond hair and his blue eyes, whereas Daisy thought he was gorgeous to look at.

"I'm spending the night with the general tonight," Daisy said with a mischievous smile.

"Well, have fun, try not to miss him for the three days we shall be gone," Kit replied sarcastically.

"Oh, I shall pine for him greatly," Daisy teased.

Kit laughed at her. "However will you cope?" she teased back.

"We all know I'm not that attached, it's good to have some fun, you know, you should try it once in a while," Daisy replied with a flick of her purple hair.

Kit simply laughed back at her whilst surveying the garden. It wasn't as if Kit hadn't had lovers before, they just didn't last that long. Men just weren't that important to her. Daisy had often told her that would change when she met the one, which always made her giggle. As if they could be truly loved when everyone feared the power they had.

Chapter Two

The Mage ran through the manor house, turning and running into more dead ends. As she let out a frustrated sigh at another blocked corridor, she turned and carried on running up the long, twisted stair case towards the manor house's tower. She thought she was never going to get out of there alive. She pushed herself to go faster taking two stairs at a time. This was the last room to try and she could hear the knight's heavy steps coming up the stairs. Her breathing was heavy. As she reached the top, she came across a heavy oak door. She tried the handle with no luck; she shoved her whole weight against the heavy door. It opened with a judder; she quickly ran inside and scanned the room for an escape route. The room was scattered with old clothes stuffed in crates, empty barrels covered in years of dust and old furniture which was no longer needed. Sunlight shone through the cracks in the roof making the dust sparkle. She grabbed an old barrel, positioned it underneath a roof beam and heaved herself on to it. She could just about reach the beam if she jumped a little. As she pulled herself on to the first beam, she managed to kick over the barrel, she had to do anything she could to try slow down the knights. This was her only chance of escape.

The kingdom had banned the use of magic and sorcery within its lands unless it was used advantageously in war in the king's name. The Mage was certainly not going to use her abilities to aid the kingdom, quite the opposite. She was part of the revolt to overthrow the kingdom and its royal family. The revolt believed that magic belonged everywhere it was a part of life; however, the royal family did not trust the powers in the very earth they walked upon. The revolt had heard of great power that lived within the walls of the castle, super warriors that were said to be half god half devil. The magic and power these individuals held would tip the odds of overthrowing the royals in the revolt's favour. The Mage had been sent on a quest to seek out these warriors, to uncover the truth behind them to see if such power was possible. However, it was this quest that had got her captured and held prisoner in the manor house.

As she reached the top beam in the roof, the knights came crashing through the door shouting and bellowing. The Mage had little choice, it was now or never. She began frantically pulling parts of the straw roof down on their heads. As the knights straightened the barrel and climbed upon it, making their way to the first beam, a sweat broke out on the Mage's forehead. The knights began to climb from one beam to another getting closer and closer. The Mage pulled down more straw, grasping handfuls and throwing them to the floor, she grazed her hand doing so wincing in pain. She didn't let it stop her. As the hole became bigger, she wriggled herself through the gap, slid down the side of the roof, ripping the side of her dress in the process and landing on the clay guttering. The Mage nearly lost her balance teetering on the side of the house; she took a deep breath of fresh air to calm her racing heart. She had to think quickly, glancing around, she decided the best way to get down was lowering herself on to the wooden balcony-like structure which ran alongside the manor. She took deep ragged breaths as she hung momentarily from the roof, the ground spinning underneath her. Once on the wooden structure she swiftly ran along the edge before jumping down gracefully and running into the forest before the knights had a chance to get through the roof.

The Mage carried on running through the forest zigzagging through the dense undergrowth past tree after tree; she jumped over fallen branches and stumbled over rocks. With every step she took, the presence of the knights faded away, she felt like she could finally breathe a sigh of relief. A small clearing in the woods provided a brief moment of rest; she had run a long way deep in to the forest where the knights would never venture due to the tales of demons and ghosts that dwelled within.

As she rested, her heart rate began to return to normal. She could feel eyes upon her, surrounding her, hidden away, watching her. She gently raised her palm to reveal a blue eye etched into her skin. The symbol of peace that every revolt member bore. The watching eyes belonged to what the kingdom called barbarians or savages. They were no more savages than anyone living on this earth today. These savages worshipped under the sorcerer Merlin, believed to be their leader. His type of magic was also banned within the kingdom, leaving them to live among the natural protection of the forest. She carried on after her short break, walking swiftly, picking her way through the forest making sure not to leave a trail behind her. The Mage was headed towards the rebel's hideout hidden on the other side of the forest behind two rock sides. The location was well concealed and if people didn't know it was there, they would never find it.

After a day of travelling the Mage finally arrived at her

destination, her hands and her dress were in a disarray, she was covered in mud and moss. She wiped her hair from her face looking down at her dishevelled appearance sighing loudly. She knocked on the wooden shack's door tentatively, trying to sort her dress out so she wasn't exposing herself. A small shutter hole within the door opened up with two beady black eyes looking down on her.

"You're late," the beady eyes barked at her from behind the door. "Sorry, Hinesta, I ran into some trouble," the Mage replied easily.

With that the door opened with a squeak of its hinges. The Mage stepped inside the dimly lit shack and followed Hinesta through to the back room.

"Ahh the great Mage returns," Alston replied with a snarky manner.

She ignored him and carried on making her way over to their leader. Their leader consisted of an older gentleman with a long beard and balding head. The Mage bowed her head slightly in acknowledgment of who he was.

"Master, I am sorry for the delayed return, I am afraid the quest failed." The Mage sat on the barrel opposite the leader, pulling her dress over her legs.

"I thought as much, what do you suggest is the next course of action?" The leader rubbed his eyes wearily.

"Well, master, I suggest a team of us go together, one isn't enough for the knights of the kingdom, and I barely made it out alive." The Mage looked intently at the leader.

The fire crackled lazily spitting embers at them. The leader rose slowly. As he turned his back towards the Mage and made his way towards the door he said, "very well, Mage, do as you see fit."

She stared at the barrel where the leader had been sitting, the fire cracked softly at the side of her. Her thoughts drifted to the first time she had met the leader of their revolt; she had been just a child then. Running through the dirty streets of Belware with a stolen hemp bag of food for the other orphans, she had run straight into the leader on his grey palace horse. At the time she had simply known him as the king's brother, second to the throne. However, soon after that day he would join them on the streets as he had been left for dead by his brother the king himself, who had personally seen to it that his brother Charles had a hunting accident. The orphans had found him and brought him to the Mage, who had nursed him back to life using her knowledge of occult magic. It had taken weeks for Charles to regain his strength. Once strong enough he became obsessed with taking the kingdom and destroying the royal family.

Chapter Three

As the waves crashed against the Viking long boat, they rocked it gently from side to side. Splashback from the waves sprayed the deck of the boat. The sun was starting to set, casting everything into gloomy shadows, as the boat headed towards the upcoming cliffs. The boat belonged to King Ake who was known to be one of the most violent Vikings in the north. His boat was known as the long serpentine with a huge engraved dragon-like head mounted on the front, the impressive feature was to scare off opposition.

The Viking King Ake had decided to conquer the kingdom of Belware to give to his three sons Bjoarn, Destin and Ethan. This allowed him to keep ruling his own kingdom without the threat of being overthrown by his eldest sons. He often feared his sons would fight over this land due to its great wealth and power, but with three young children and another child on the way he had little choice but to expand his family's rule to other lands. He knew they would make great leaders as they were strong, fearless, good warriors and had good judgement for right and wrong.

However, he was mildly concerned about the rumours, whispers and mutterings he had heard about god-like creatures which roamed this land, he hoped for his son's sake that they were just that, rumours. The water that surrounded the long boat started to get shallower. King Ake signalled to the men to stop rowing and then cut the rope holding the anchor upon the boat. The heavy chain groaned with the weight of the anchor as it fell into the water with a mighty splash. One by one the Vikings jumped out of the boat holding fur bags full of weapons and essential items that would be vital for their survival.

Destin, the second eldest son of King Ake brought up the rear of the Viking procession, he glanced up at the cliffs over shadowing the beach they were currently trekking along. As he looked up, he could have sworn he had seen a man with a blue torso stood at the very edge of the cliff, he shook his head and looked again, this time the man had disappeared. As he stared at the edge of the cliff, blinking his eyes rapidly, he wondered what special power this land really held as he too had heard of the magic kept in the palace walls; however he thought that magic was a tale told to small children to keep them out of trouble. He took his eyes away from the cliffs and carried on walking, head lowered, bracing himself against the wind battering into them. His eldest brother was in front of him muttering to himself.

"Bjoarn, did you see that on the clifftop?" Destin asked glancing back at the cliffs. "You getting spooked?" Bjoarn laughed at his younger brother.

Destin snorted. "Of course not, I just thought I saw a blue man."

"You're tired, your eyes are playing tricks," Bjoarn replied with an exasperated tone.

Destin didn't reply, he didn't want to anger his brother but he became more and more certain that he had indeed seen something.

The Vikings headed up the coastal path towards the

clifftop and into the huge forest which lay in front of them, the king had decided they were to set up camp for the night under the shelter of the ancient trees. The trees were huge and sprawling with the vast forest covering miles of land. The procession had walked miles into the depth of the forest under the cover of darkness. Eventually the Vikings found a clearing which was big enough for the many men King Ake had brought on the voyage. Destin settled down with his two brothers beside one of the crackling fires which had been made from fallen branches, they all huddled around them to keep themselves warm. Gruel was being served by the few servants brought on the exhibition to keep the king comfortable. As Destin ate his portion of gruel, he kept getting an uneasy feeling in the pit of his gut, now and again he looked into the trees, craning his neck to see if he could see the tree tops. With the amount of leaf coverage and the cloak of darkness enveloping everything it was impossible.

"Bjoarn?" he asked, in hushed tones, shifting his gaze to his brother.

"Yes?" Bjoarn answered eating his gruel sloppily.

"I have a feeling we are being watched," Destin said as he put the bowl down and twisted his body towards the trees.

An arrow came shooting down from within the trees narrowly missing them; another followed an inch away from Bjoarn's foot. More arrows came raining down upon them, men cried out in pain as they were hit. But with all this happening Destin couldn't tear himself away from staring into the trees, until he saw startling white eyes set inside a blue face staring back at him, he gasped in surprise and he made a grab for Bjoarn's arm but missed as his brother had already leapt up and was quickly reaching for his weapons.

"We're under attack!" Bjoarn shouted.

Destin looked around in bewilderment as every man that wasn't injured was trying to fire arrows back at the unseen enemy, shielding themselves or trying to climb up the trees. He could hear faint chanting among the rustling of leaves; the wind appeared from nowhere swirling around their feet. Destin didn't know which way to look, what to do or how to get out of this haunted forest. The Vikings couldn't see their opponents but they could definitely feel their wrath. More cries of the slain were echoing around them. When Bjoarn grabbed Destin's arm and tugged him towards the edge of the clearing, they stumbled over the dead, over the fires and instruments they had brought with them. Some of the men were trying to pick up belongings whilst shielding themselves from arrows; some were still trying to fight back with arrows and swords; whilst others were running blindly into the forest. After several minutes of fighting, the unseen enemy, King Ake, made the decision they couldn't fight what they couldn't see.

"Move out!" the king shouted over the chaos before him.

The remaining Vikings made a dash for the cover of the trees, they raced through the forest with the unseen enemy following them chanting, firing arrows with the wind blowing through the trees turning everything sinister around the group. As they reached the edge of the forest breathing heavy sweat dripping in their eyes, Bjoarn looked at Destin with confusion as they stood in a sprawling field.

"What in the world was that?" Bjoarn asked bent over catching his breath. Destin stole a glance at the forest.

"Could it be haunted?" Ethan, their youngest brother, asked placing his belongings in a fur bag.

"I saw the blue man again," Destin said looking at Bjoarn. As Bjoarn started to tell Destin there was no such thing as blue men. King Ake interrupted their exchange.

"I must confess something to you all," the king spoke with earnest in his voice. The king's men all gathered around him to listen to what was about to be said.

"This land is known to hold great power, it is said that there are god and demon like creatures roaming among the people, the forest, and on the very earth we stand on." The king paused and looked down for a second. "I should have told you about the danger of coming on this voyage as it is like no other, we have ever dared."

The men were silent, shifting only slightly from foot to foot, staring at their King. Destin felt annoyance flare up within him, he had been on many raids in the past but never like this, never fighting unseen enemies with god-like power.

"If this land, this kingdom, is powerful, this means it has wealth, riches and prospects for every man here. We are here to claim them and we shall not fail!" Bjoarn said with defiance.

With that the king looked at his eldest son with pride, he placed his hand on his shoulder and he knew from that moment he had not made a mistake bringing his sons here.

Destin's eyebrows arched as he heard his brother speak, he couldn't quite believe what he was hearing and almost shook his head in disbelief, and he turned away from the group staring at the forest watching for any movement. Out of the corner of his eye he saw blue movement. He gulped deeply.

Chapter Four

As the sun shone through the chamber's stained-glass windows Kits eye fluttered open. As she stared at the ceiling, she let out a sigh. She managed to roll herself out of bed even though she didn't want to leave the warmth of the blanket. She stood up with a stretch of her neck and back. As she went to get dressed, she had an uneasy feeling in the pit of her stomach. As she placed her cloak over her shoulders, she tried to shake off that feeling. She had decided to wear her fur cloak today which clung to the ground; the gold medallion which hung from the cloak signified her ranking in the army. Not at the top but close. She had served for almost ten years, the legal minimum amount of time required. As she wound her long straight white hair into a bun her mind wandered off into her future. When she was alone, she often let herself day dream of what life would be like out of the army. What it would be like to be a normal woman, not that she would ever really experience that now. She had managed to save a lot of silver which she was hoping would buy a small farm, where she could have some animals and live without rules and regulations, where she could do as she pleased.

A knock on her door brought her back into the present. Before she could say enter Daisy burst through the door. Kit couldn't help but smile at her. They were so different in how they looked, Daisy was very short and curvy with vibrant purple hair which was hard to miss, whereas Kit was taller than Daisy but not too tall for a woman. She was lean with startling white hair which hung almost to the bottom of her back when it was down. But their personalities were very similar which is why they got on so well, bouncing off of each other.

"Guess what I did last night?" Daisy asked with a slight smirk and a sparkle in her eyes.

"Hmm let me guess." Kit paused for a second "sneak around the castle after the general?" she asked, laughing at Daisy whilst adjusting her hair.

"Of course, what else is there to do in this godforsaken castle?" Daisy asked, with a raise of her eyebrows, leaning against the stone wall of the chamber.

Kit laughed and shook her head at her as they made their way through the chamber door.

"Honestly you should find yourself a man Kit; surely you want to get married at some point?" Daisy asked her, walking through stone archways.

Kit thought for a second. "No, I'm not into the obligation of marriage and the rules that need to be followed. Look at the princess, for instance, marrying someone she doesn't love for her country, it's not for me."

"The general doesn't want to get married. He told me last night, so we can be spinsters together." Daisy laughed.

"Doesn't sound like the worst thing to be honest," Kit mused with an arched eyebrow. "Speak for yourself," Daisy said mockingly, eyeing Kit up and down.

"Anyway, what about that soldier you were dating?" Daisy asked as they made their way out of the castle to wait for the princess in the vast court yard.

Kit sighed. "We were not compatible."

Daisy chuckled to herself, "Meaning what exactly?"

Kit thought for a moment. "I honestly think he was scared of me."

"That age old problem of a strong woman intimidating men," Daisy said. "How pathetic." She giggled.

"At the moment I don't want to date, I'm too busy concentrating on my studies," Kit said, straightening her spine.

"What have you taught yourself recently?" Daisy asked in a hushed tone, looking around to make sure no one was around.

"How to heal, it's so interesting, I use different plants to get different effects," Kit said excitedly.

"With training to fight, looking after Puzat, and then studying magic no wonder you're too busy for a man." Daisy laughed at Kit.

Kit glanced at Daisy for a brief second but Kit knew she had a point, hiding in her chamber all night wasn't going to help with the issue of people being scared of her.

Elegant carriages were parked around the courtyard waiting for the ladies in waiting who always joined the princess Nekite where ever she went. Kit always thought of them as shadows just following, never really speaking, just scurrying behind the princess. There were five in total and Kit only knew their names, nothing much else about them. Daisy didn't like the one called Eva: she spoke to them badly, always making demands as if she was the princess herself. Kit let it wash over her, always daydreaming of a time when she would be out of this place, however Daisy found it incredibly difficult to ignore Eva. Eva liked to remind Daisy she came from a whorehouse, she was the only one that dared speak to them, trying to taunt them and provoking a reaction from them.

Several times Kit had to pull Daisy to the side to remind her not to step out of her place.

When they had arrived at this kingdom with no money and no idea where they were, Daisy made the decision they needed money and quick. A sign hung up haphazardly outside the whorehouse which read WANTED DANCERS, they had never danced before it wasn't something done in the laboratory or their home towns but with their ability to learn quickly and their powers which were used lightly, they became good at putting on shows. Shows which people had never seen before, people from far and wide came to watch the girls, dance. Their new found popularity spread through the kingdom until it reached the ears of the general, he had stormed the whorehouse with a handful of knights to take down this power brewing within. However, the knights came up against something unexpected, half god half devils, from that point in time Kit and Daisy had become soldiers.

Chapter Five

Princess Nekite stared at herself in the mirror, twisting her head from side to side to see her whole reflection. Beauty stared back at her. The dim candle light caught her molten brown eyes flickering with innocence and hope for her future. She curled her jet-black hair into a plaited bun, setting it in place with pearls and gold clips which looked like stars against the dark night. Her thoughts drifted to her future husband and the upcoming wedding. Her heart began to skip a few beats as her future husband was to be Prince Geoffrey of the neighbouring kingdom Carak. He was tall, handsome and said to be brave in battle, but as the princess sat pinning her hair in place a thought struck her that she definitely did not love him. It felt like her heart plummeted within her. When she had spoken with her mother about this matter, she had been reassured that love would come in time. Nekite hoped this was the case as she yearned for feeling of pure love that she had heard about in ancient tales that her grandmother had told her when she was a little girl. It was due to this yearning feeling of love and the uncertainty of her future husband she had come up with a compromise. She knew her duty was to unite the two kingdoms to create peace, therefore she would never disobey her parents, but she also had to have an input into her future. The compromise was agreed at weekly chaperoned meetings with Prince Geoffrey, this gave her a fair chance to get to know him and maybe just maybe fall in love with him. A faint knock on her chamber door brought her round from her thoughts. She sighed with discontent and pushed herself up from her stool.

"Enter," she said in a regal clipped tone.

Four of her ladies in waiting entered the chamber doing a curtsey before standing before the princess.

"Your majesty, Eva is unwell, she has been advised to rest instead of taking the journey to Carak with us today," Alice stated in a matter-of-fact tone.

The princess frowned slightly. "Oh, I hope she is okay?" she asked still frowning as Eva had seemed fine yesterday during cross stitch. An illness to come on this quick wasn't ideal and the princess hoped it wasn't too serious as Eva was an important part of the wedding ceremony. She then scolded herself for thinking about herself instead of Eva's health.

"Oh yes, your majesty, the medicine woman says she just needs good rest," Alice replied cutting into the princess's thoughts.

"Well in that case I am sure she will be well for our return," Nekite said with a smile. "Shall we?" she said nodding towards the door.

The princess led the ladies in waiting out of her chamber along the corridors and outside into the courtyard where she spotted Kit and Daisy standing outside her carriage. The princess was slightly apprehensive of the guards, the rumours she had heard terrified her, she was sure that was why her dad had assigned them to protect her, to stop her disobeying their rules, she wouldn't dare anyway. As she stood staring at the guards who were chatting away to themselves, the ladies in waiting were giggling excitedly next to her. The princess knew they hoped to meet future suitors for themselves; the men in this kingdom were boring, well, she assumed from what she had heard. She sighed to herself as she listened to the excited chatter surrounding her, even the guards looked happy. As she stood there, she wished her life wasn't so bound with obligation. She strolled towards her impressive carriage, adorned with golden and cream fixtures with four gleaming white horses in front of it, with the royal coat of arms proudly emblazoned on the side. She nodded at the guards as they opened the door for her; she hitched up her heavily embroidered dress and stepped inside the red silk interior. Her ladies in waiting filed in after her. Once they were seated and comfortable, they resumed their chatting. The carriage pulled off with pebbles spraying from the wheel.

"Your majesty, how are you finding the prince?" Linota asked, settling herself down.

After a moment of thought Nekite answered, "I have to marry him regardless of how I feel."

"I think he's dreamy!" exclaimed Bela, then her eyes widened and she placed a hand over her mouth whilst Alice, Linota and Rosia all laughed at her.

"Sorry, your majesty, I shouldn't have spoken out of turn." Nekite chuckled at her and waved a hand at her.

"Bela its fine, you can express how you feel, we are friends here!" Nekite exclaimed. "And he is handsome, I agree with you, the only problem is I haven't had that spark," she said wistfully, glancing out of the window.

"Doesn't that spark come over time?" Bela said, trying to sound convincing.

"That was my reasoning for meeting him over a period of time; I am indeed very lucky and grateful for my parents to allow me to do so," she replied.

Nekite was very aware that most noble women were often forced into arranged marriages without any say. She was very lucky her parents were so kind regarding this matter. Her mother had told her it was because she had only been blessed with one child, therefore the queen had gone about spoiling her rotten. However, this still didn't seem enough to Nekite, she often thought she was greedy and should just be content with what life had to offer. She glanced out of the window again to see Kit and Daisy astride their horses, busy chatting away to one another. She sighed again, turned around, and engaged in the conversation inside the carriage.

"You are indeed smart for coming up with such an idea," Alice said with approval.

The other ladies in waiting nodded in agreement. Nekite didn't think so but she thanked and agreed with them regardless.

Chapter Six

Kit and Daisy rode alongside the majestic carriage side by side, keeping an eye on the princess who kept glancing out of the window. Kit was astride her horse which she had called Puzat. He was thought of as a common horse due to his coat pattern being brown and white. But he was braver and more fearless than most warriors Kit had fought alongside. He had been beside her in every battle. Whereas Daisy rode her black mare which she called Demon that had also been in battle after battle. Kit and Puzat shared a secret that no one other than Daisy knew; it created a bond so strong it couldn't be broken.

Other soldiers and warriors didn't understand and often laughed at the expense of Kit. She didn't care though, they were not her friends. They didn't ask her to go to the tavern with them, or to train with them, and therefore she had very little concern to what they thought about her. They had not been through hell like Kit had been, and once you have lived in hell it takes a little part of who you are.

The bond that would never be broken between Kit and Puzat came down to one very bloody battle. Many died that day, many injured and many not able to return to normal life. Kit herself was badly injured and Puzat killed.

Since becoming a soldier her interest in sorcery and magic grew. She would study late into the night under the dim lights of the candles. The lotions, potions and Latin chants fascinated her and whoever created them had always intrigued her. Kit owned lots of Celtic and Druid scrolls which she studied night after night. Kit's psychological and bodily modifications aided her in the hobby of magic, making it very easy for her to learn. The first piece of sorcery she had harnessed was the control of weather, suddenly bringing out the sun, the wind or the rain whenever she felt like it. Creating electric storms by conducting energy through the metal-like claws that protruded through her skin, she didn't like getting them out as they ripped through her skin like knives. However, rubbing those metal claws together could create sparks which she turned into fire. She admitted to herself, when she was on the battlefield she must look like the devil himself. From there she had studied astral magic: the moon, stars and the sun phases creating different formulas she could use to her advantage. All the magic chants and rituals were written in Latin, which was a second language to Kit. This was from her life in the laboratory when languages would be useful when in foreign lands. The darkest magic Kit had learnt was the revival of the dead. This was as far as she would delve into the dark side, she admitted to Daisy that is scared her a little the power she could have. At first Daisy thought she was crazy for studying magic at all, never mind the dark stuff. But on the day of that battle Kit couldn't be more grateful of the art she had harnessed.

An arrow embedded into Kit's shoulder caused searing pain through her entire body making moving difficult. Blood soaked through her shirt, grit stung her eyes and a deep wound cut across her stomach. As Puzat lay dying in her arms from four arrows in his chest she made a decision that changed the course of fate. She told herself she owed it to him; he had saved her life more than any other soldier she had fought alongside.

To most people he was just a horse, but to Kit he was her protector, her soldier, one of her best friends.

However, achieving the unthinkable was difficult. When practicing this dark magic in the safety of her chamber it was done on mice or frogs she had come across, performing this ritual on a full-sized horse was a different matter. She remembered crying out in anguish as he took his last breath, amidst the arrows flying past her, soldiers crying out in pain, her claws fully extended from her hand she drew a magic circle with the blood from her enemies. This circle enclosed her and the dead horse. She drew various symbols stating what was to be done. She dragged one injured soldier into the circle, this was an exchange, a life for a life. The onslaught of rain drove into her blurring her vision. She began repeatedly chanting the ancient words, as she did so she stabbed the soldier in his chest, ripping his beating heart from within. She cut some of her hair, soaking it with blood as she did so. Kit wrapped the piece of hair around the heart and around Puzat's leg. She carried on chanting, getting faster and faster until it was a frenzy of words. The ground shook beneath her, the circle whizzed around her, blurred, the blue eyes shone like torches. Shadows climbed through the cracks, taking the heart and soldier from her hands, replacing it with another one. That day she changed the course of life and death. She became even more powerful than she would ever realise.

Chapter Seven

The Vikings raided village after village, settlement after settlement and whatever was left in between. They were ruthless, fierce and unforgiving to anyone that stood in their way. As they swept through the kingdom the Vikings collected riches, silks, linen and any animal that proved useful. The king ordered them to replace what was lost to them in the forest.

Even though they had been unbeaten in the many raids since coming to the kingdom, Destin still felt uneasy and shaken up. He couldn't quite get rid of this feeling frequently looking over his shoulder.

"Will you stop doing that," Bjoarn told Destin.

"It's a habit," Destin retorted.

"From the forest?" Bjoarn asked. "You have to forget that, look how successful we have been since," Bjoarn said, looking around at their riches.

Destin scanned his eyes around the spoils. "I know, I know, However I still feel like we're being watched."

Bjoarn let out an exasperated sigh. Ethan laughed at them both.

"Is Destin spooked?" Ethan laughed, clapping Destin on the back.

"I am son of King Ake. I don't get spooked," Destin said with authority he didn't feel. His brothers laughed at him whilst walking away shaking their heads.

Destin watched as they both walked away laughing to themselves, his brows creased together shaking his head.

That night they camped next to a river, they were to stay there for a few days, the king had ordered them to rest and enjoy their free time. Some of the men wandered off to nearby towns in search of taverns and women, whereas Destin had decided to stay near camp, still not trusting the land. He gathered his woollen and linen shirts and took them to the river's edge to clean them, one shirt in particular had a few blood stains and they were proving hard to get out. He didn't know why he was bothering to clean it when he could afford more shirts with the amount of gold, silver and jewels he had raided but it got him away from the other men and he could relax a little. As he sat next to the river, listening to the rush of water over stones and pebbles, he could see his reflection staring back at him, his long plaited hair over one shoulder, piercing blue eyes and a small beard he looked every part of being a Viking but most of the time he felt like an imposter. He went to grab another shirt, whilst doing so he glanced up to see a woman stood opposite him across the river, an eagle perched on her shoulder.

"Hello?" Destin shouted.

The woman looked at him with surprise; she then suddenly started to turn away. "No don't go, what is your name? "Destin tried again.

The woman carried on turning and rushed into the forest behind her without saying a word. Destin muttered to himself, "There is something not right with this place."

He kept his eyes on the opposite side of the river where the woman had been standing whilst he gathered his belongings. He rushed backed to the main campsite where his brothers had returned with two deer slung over their shoulders.

"I saw a girl," Destin said breathlessly. Bjoarn and Ethain looked at each other with raised eyebrows. They placed the deer near the fire.

"Was she beautiful?" Bjoarn asked, laughing. "Was she blue?" Ethan joined in.

Destin looked at them both, exasperated.

"No, she was just an ordinary girl, but why was she out here all alone? There must be more in the forest." He tried not to sound nervous.

Bjoarn hesitated for a second, mulling the information over. "If Destin is correct then we must be careful, we are to be the only ones, raiding."

The other men cheered him on, as they sat down near the fire ready to skin the deer for the feast that night.

Chapter Eight

The Mage quickened her pace into the forest, not daring to look back, as she hurried through the forest her thoughts went to the strange man by the river. Who was he, where did he come from and what was he doing? She guessed with only two towns to go before the kingdom it was more than likely his destination. She shook her head, she didn't really have time to ponder on it as she had a team of revolt members to sort out. She and Alston had devised a plan of action which was to be implemented when the princess travelled to Carak. They would carry out a surprise attack on the carriages, but the Mage had stressed to the members of the revolt that no one was to be harmed, as they just needed the god-like creatures. She walked out of the forest, whispered to the eagle perched on her hand and let him fly. She placed a hand over her eyes to shield them from the sun as she watched the bird soar through the sky. She muttered the ritualistic words and her eyes turned from green to black. Instantly she could see what the bird could see which was treetops, the river and nearby mountains.

She was going to have the majestic bird fly towards the palace to see if the princess was en route yet, but before she did this she had to see if that man was still at the river. She was just too curious. She circled the bird round and it flew towards where she had been standing. As the bird flew close, she had it land in a nearby tree. From that vantage point she could see a campsite with many men milling around within. The Mage picked out the man who had been down at the river. He was standing next to two other men who looked similar to him. The men looked different from the men in Belware. Long hair, beards and lots of jewels adorned them. She was mildly concerned at why they were here but she had a job to do. She had the bird fly out of the tree and along the river towards the palace.

As she was busy concentrating on the bird, she didn't appear to notice Alston walk up behind her.

"Boo," he said, grabbing her waist.

"Get off, I'm busy," she said with irritation lacing her words.

"Did I scare you?" he mocked.

"Of course not, I could hear you coming miles away, you're as quiet as a rampaging boar!" the Mage exclaimed, with a smile.

"How rude." He laughed with mock hurt.

"True." She laughed at him.

"Have you found them yet?" he asked, pulling himself back together.

"Nothing as of yet, I doubt they have set off yet," she said, concentrating on the bird's view.

"Yes, it's early, being that beautiful must take ages to get ready," he said with a smile.

"Anyone can be beautiful when they have beautiful things!" she said haughtily.

"Are you jealous," he mocked her again.

"Of course not, I just think she has an unfair advantage," the Mage said with a softer tone.

Aston looked at her, he found her beautiful, and her green eyes enchanted him. Her short choppy hair looked adorable and her scruffy clothes didn't make her look dumpy like it did with the other woman in the revolt. However, he would never admit it to anyone.

"I think the lady protests too much," he mocked again.

She went to swipe him but he dodged out of her reach, tripped over a stone and fell on his back. She stood laughing at him.

"Will you please let me concentrate?" She laughed.

"Sorry mam," he mocked.

The Mage rolled her eyes, turned around and concentrated on what she could see. She could sense Alston next to her. They stood there for a further ten minutes until the Mage suddenly let out a squeal of delight.

"I've found them, I've found them!" She jumped up and down. "We need to get the horses," Aston said.

"They're just joining the south track straight out of the palace gates," she said with excitement.

She said the ritual and her eyes returned to their normal green, they rushed into the forest, running into the clearing to join the others.

"The princess and the guards are joining the south track, if we ride hard, we can ambush them at creek's pass." Aston informed the others.

The members of the revolt mounted their ponies and set off at a canter towards the north, it wouldn't take them long to reach where the princess was. Alston had picked the creek's pass for the ambush as they would be hidden from sight high up in the rocky mountain terrain but would have a good vantage point.

The first part of the plan was to throw huge nets over the guards at the front and back of the carriage, hopefully rendering them useless. The second part of the plan was to isolate the god-like creatures, and talk them round, to make them see their point of view.

They reached the pass in plenty of time, the revolt members started to scurry around. One hid the horses around the back of the rocky terrain, tying them to a tree. And one started to drag the huge nets up the tiny path to the vantage point where Alston and the Mage were sitting.

"Do you think this will work?" The Mage looked out anxiously over the track below them. "Of course, I have planned every last detail," he said with pride in his voice.

"I'm not doubting you, I'm just anxious, this is our only chance at this." The Mage furrowed her brow.

"Stop worrying, I have everything under control, you know we can do this," he said comfortably.

She smiled at him. "You're right, I'm actually a little excited to see what they look like."

"I bet they have horns growing from their head and are surrounded by fire." He chuckled at her shocked expression.

"I'm joking." He laughed at her.

The Mage wasn't sure how they would tackle the god-like creatures, the other guards were easy to handle, and the revolt had certain battle skills, like sword fighting and archery, which would greatly aid them. However, the Mage doubted very much they could take on gods. They all waited anxiously behind the rocky terrain, listening for the sound of horses to approach, quietly chatting to one another.

"I have a bad feeling in the pit of my stomach." The Mage looked down at her dress which she was nervously playing with.

"I thought you were fearless?" Alston asked scanning the track.

"No one is fearless." She sighed. "I feel bad spirits are surrounding this place is all." She shrugged and forced herself to stop playing with the hem of her dress.

He placed his hand on hers to try and reassure her. Before he could speak the sound of hooves filled the air. He quickly let go and reached for his net. The Mage checked she had her knife tucked under her dress, and then grabbed her net. She peered through the gap in the rocks to see a magnificent carriage drawn by four sparkling horses. She gasped at the sight. This was the moment that would change the future. She went to stand up, but as she did her eyes locked with one of the god-like creatures, she was mesmerized by what she saw. The god-like creature was a woman, which surprised the Mage as she had assumed they would be men, and she was also shocked by the solid bright blue eyes which were staring at her. She assumed they were staring at her. She couldn't quite tell, however, as the eyes had no pupils, no iris, just solid blue pools. The hair, completely white, flowing down her back was a stark contrast from her eyes. She could see metal claws emerge from the creature's hand; the claws were as long as butcher's knives piercing the skin. As she stood staring at her the Mage was vaguely aware of the revolt members running down the rocky path towards them, she was also aware of the sound of thundering horse hooves coming from the other direction. Alston went to throw his net.

"Alston no!" she shouted at him tearing her eyes away from the god.

Chapter Nine

Kit had seen the people in the terrain above them before they had bothered to stand up. She had tilted her head slightly so that Daisy was made aware of them. She could see some of the people, who looked like paupers to her, run down a rocky path to their side.

"I don't know why they try," Daisy said with a shake of her head. Her metal fangs protruded through her gums to half way down her neck.

Kit just shrugged and shouted, "Stop the carriage." They saw a net come flying down.

"Guards, protect the carriage!" Daisy shouted.

Kit and Daisy turned their horses away from the carriage making sure they wouldn't get caught up in the nets.

The nets flew down entangling the guards beneath, rendering them useless. Kit looked at Daisy with a raised eyebrow. Her focus was not on the scruffy paupers above but the sound of the many thundering hooves ahead.

"Seriously, on our last day?" Daisy asked with an exasperated tone.

"You wanted a battle to end your soldier career," Kit retorted back with a laugh. Daisy smiled back, the black mare was becoming restless beneath her.

"I don't like the sound up ahead," Daisy said trying to stop the mare from rearing.

"Doesn't sound good, definitely an ambush with a lot of men, whatever happens we protect the princess," Kit replied halting Puzat, who seemed calm in comparison to Daisy's steed.

"So we dismount, hide, then attack?" Daisy asked, letting go of the reins, swinging her leg over the saddle and landing gracefully on the floor.

"I take the right, you take the left," Kit replied, dismounting as well.

"Princess, I would advise you stay in the carriage," Daisy said, popping her head through the carriage door.

The princess nodded her head at Daisy; she looked as white as a ghost.

Kit cut four of the guards free from their traps. "Guard the princess with your lives. Puzat, hide within the near trees I will call when I need you," Kit whispered into his ear, gave him a quick rub on the neck and ran towards the opening of the track.

The sound of the hooves got louder as they hurried to hide themselves within the brash of the forest. The other guards were still entangled, the ladies in waiting in the carriage and the paupers running towards the snared guards.

"The princess is scared, I doubt she has ever seen anything like this before," Daisy lowered her head into the brash.

"No, she won't have, she will be fine though, something to talk to the prince about," Kit replied.

As Daisy nodded in agreement, dozens of black horses charged through the opening of the track, with soldiers dressed in red. Kit couldn't make out their faces as red devil masks covered their expressions making them faceless. Kit gasped at the sight of it. Daisy's face mirrored confusion.

"We run, jump and mount the last horses," Kit mouthed at Daisy.

She nodded back, and they crept out of the brash silently, hunched down, and ran as fast as they could to catch the last galloping horse. As they caught up to the horses, they both swiftly leapt off their feet, somersaulted in the air and gracefully landed on the back of the horses behind the warriors.

Daisy took one bite from the warrior's neck and threw him to the floor. She moved herself into the saddle. The red warriors had halted and were slaying the paupers as they tried to run. Kit sliced through the neck of the warrior with ease, threw him on the ground and rode the horse to Daisy.

"The carriage!" Daisy shouted.

The red warriors were slaughtering the king's guards who were trying to free the other guards from the nets whilst surrounding the carriage in a bid to protect the princess.

"We must protect the princess!" Kit shouted back.

"Yes, the guards don't stand a chance," Daisy shouted back slicing through a red warrior with her sword.

Kit whispered Puzat's name and he came charging out of the forest straight into a red warrior heading towards them, the horse was knocked over and the rider thrown to the ground. Kit rode past and placed an axe in the warrior's chest.

A horse collided into Daisy, the rider trying to kill her, she quickly stabbed him in the leg and, as he screamed out in surprise, she grabbed his shirt, pulled him close and bit his neck. Blood dripped from her metal fangs and rolled down her neck staining her white shirt.

Kit jumped off the horse, as a warrior lunged at her with a sword which she easily side-stepped. She grabbed the sword with her claws, pulling it towards her bringing the warrior with it. She stabbed him in his heart, blood spurted out covering her.

As she sliced through another warrior's neck, she looked

over at the carriage. The ladies in waiting were being dragged out and forced onto the ground.

"We need to get to the princess," Kit shouted over at Daisy.

"It's not like I'm not trying," Daisy retorted, pulling her knife from a warrior's back.

Kit could see a pauper slide under the carriage towards the princess. Three men came towards Kit with their swords ready; she let them get close before she dropped to the ground, leg out to the right, she spun round kicking one of them over. She sprang off her feet, launched herself at another warrior with her left arm up, defending herself from his sword, whilst her right arm with the claws at full length cut his throat almost to the bone. She spun round quickly, just missing an axe from the final one. She smiled to herself, rotated herself again, high kicked him in the face and, as he dropped to the floor, she cartwheeled over him impaling him with her claws.

The Mage hid behind a rock, looking at the carnage in front of her. She couldn't see Alston anywhere. She hoped he was okay. The red warriors were rounding up the guards and executing them at the front of the carriage. As she looked over the rocks, she could see the princess was being forced around the other side of the carriage being held hostage with the guards. She had to get her out of here. She dropped to the ground, half crouched half ran towards where they were. She crawled underneath the carriage heading towards the princess.

By the time the Mage had crawled in the grit and dirt towards the princess, the red warriors had finished with the guards and had begun executing the ladies in waiting, first up was Bela. They forced her onto her knees; she was crying and pleading for her life. The Mage couldn't bear the sound of it, she too began to silently weep. Just as they swung an axe into her neck, the Mage tapped the princess on the ankle. As the princess looked down the Mage placed a finger on her lips to signify quiet. The tears ran silently down the princess's face as she nodded silently. Just as the princess looked back up, the god-like creature locked eyes with the Mage, she was nodding at her as she sliced through another warrior's neck. She quickly drew her arm in under the carriage just in time as one of the warriors picked another lady.

"Why are you doing this?" the princess quietly said to the warrior stood guarding her.

"No need to worry your pretty little head over it, it will all soon be over." The devil mask laughed at her.

Just as the tears began to flow freely down her face, an axe flew through the sky, embedding itself in the neck of the warrior mocking the princess. Blood poured from the neck, seeping into the ground, running under the carriage and soaking the Mage. Before the princess could scream, the Mage grabbed her ankles. The princess dropped to the floor and the Mage dragged her under the carriage.

"We must be quiet," the Mage ushered the words. The princess nodded her head. "Follow me, we shall head towards the rocks." The Mage pointed towards the left.

The princess followed the Mage, crawling through Bela's blood, the princess stifled a scream. As the Mage stood up she checked the coast was clear and beckoned the princess up. She looked around the carriage to see the god-like creatures massacring more soldiers.

"Your Majesty, keep your head down and follow me," the Mage whispered, leading the way.

Chapter Ten

The princess followed the Mage up the rocky path hidden partially with bushes; she caught glimpses of the god-like creatures slaying the red warriors. Her mind raced wildly, what if they defeated the gods? She could feel her heart beat pounding erratically. She shook her head slightly as she noticed the Mage had started talking to her.

"Stay on the path, there's a hidden alcove on the left up ahead, I think we will be safe there," the Mage informed her.

As they reached the alcove the princess could see nets, food and handmade weapons. Panic started to rise within her.

"Who are you?" she asked the Mage in a high voice.

She made sure to keep her distance, staying near the opening of the alcove. The Mage, who had begun collecting items and putting them in a fur bag, looked up at the princess.

"Please keep the opening covered with that ivy curtain. It will stop us being seen." She sighed.

"Who are you?" the princess asked again, moving slightly.

The Mage paused for a second, contemplating what to say.

"You deserve to know the truth, I am the Mage and I am a member of the revolt," she looked down. "However, those red warriors are nothing to do with us; I don't know anything about them."

The princess looked at her, not sure whether to believe her or not, scepticism written across her face.

"It's the truth, your majesty, in actual fact we only wanted the god-like creatures as we need them to join the revolt to overthrow the king." The Mage then stood up after letting out a deep sigh.

Silence descended, the princess deep in thought trying to process the Mage's words.

"If that is the case and you are telling the truth I have some questions," the princess replied, moving away from the ivy curtain.

"Yes, your Majesty." The Mage simply nodded.

"For one, please call me Nekite." The princess settled herself on a rock.

"Why is there a revolt in the kingdom and why would this revolt want to overthrow my dad?" she looked down at the blood-soaked dress.

There was a very short pause before the Mage blurted out. "Are you seriously that ignorant? Have you not seen how the people are living? In fact, how we are not living how we are barely surviving?" The Mage frowned.

The princess's eyes widened. "No one has ever spoken to me like that."

"Well, it's about time, I'm sorry, your majesty, but this kingdom is seriously struggling and we need help. That is why there is a revolt," the Mage said, softening her frown slightly.

"What do the revolt do then, for instance, how does it help?" she asked, picking at her dress.

"The leader of the revolt was betrayed by the king, he is your uncle, your majesty." The Mage started to collect more belongings.

"He is dead, he died when I was a little girl, I can barely remember him," the princess said in a flat tone whilst frowning at the Mage.

The Mage let out a sigh.

"You won't believe me but the king, your father, is guilty of attempted murder, it is only due to the fact I found him that he is alive today," the Mage said with anger lacing her words.

"He wouldn't do that!" The princess started to raise her voice. The Mage glanced around their surroundings.

"We need to be quiet; I have been honest with you, princess, you have no reason to not believe me," the Mage said in a hushed voice.

"I just can't believe it," the princess trailed off her eyes welled up with tears. "You don't think he has anything to do with this do you?" the princess asked in a small scared voice.

The Mage simply shrugged her shoulder.

The princess was quiet for some time whilst the Mage busied herself, after collecting her thoughts she stated with more confidence than she felt, "No, he needs me to marry Prince Geoffrey."

"In that case it will be someone who wants to stop that happening," the Mage pointed out, her head cocked to the side looking directly at the princess.

The princess looked away, racking her brain for who might be behind this, but her mind kept coming up blank. She just couldn't think of anyone.

The Mage stood up, placed her bag over her shoulder and said, "I suggest we go to the revolt's hideout, we will be safe there."

"What about my guards?" the princess said. She blinked away tears. She was starting to become overwhelmed.

This was meant to be a nice final meeting before the wedding; she was going to even kiss him this time. But now she was stood in a dark damp cave with a girl who was trying to overthrow her dad as the king. She placed a hand on her chest in an effort to calm her erratic heartbeat.

Chapter Eleven

Kit stood on the track beside Daisy, covered in blood, surrounded with dead bodies, their devil masks hanging off their fallen faces. Her claws started to retract within her hands sending a sharp piercing pain through her. She could see Daisy just stood there in bewilderment, looking at the king's guards and the helpless ladies in waiting who had died today, it was simply slaughter. Kit knew that two of the ladies had run off into the woods so she was hoping they would be okay and found alive.

"We need to find the princess," Daisy said, picking her way around the bodies.

"She's with one of the paupers, they went up that rocky path." Kit pointed towards the path.

As they both stared at the path with jagged boulders and leafy overgrown plants, Kit heard a wail from underneath a red warrior. She made her way towards the sound, picking her way around the dead bodies and the puddles of blood, trying not to step in anything. As she approached the sound, she could see a very badly injured warrior lying underneath another dead body. She pulled the dead warrior off the man, an axe buried in his shoulder almost severing it from his body, blood pouring from it and another deep slash to his stomach gaped open in a half moon shape.

"Help me," the warrior said with a slow dry voice.

"I'm sorry this happened," Kit said as she felt a nudge from Puzat on her back. "Help me," the warrior repeated.

Kit looked up to see Daisy going through the dead warrior's possessions, her horse grazing on the bushes nearby and Puzat loyally next to her but no signs of other life just the sound of the wind.

"What is your name and who sent you?" Kit asked, holding the man's head up so he didn't choke on his own blood.

"My name is Tazuk, I was sent by Lady Eva Billingham from the palace," the man coughed at kit.

Kit frowned at him. "Are you sure? What was her purpose?"

"She wants the throne," he spluttered.

Kit held his head as his eyes faded and his heartbeat stopped, she placed him on the ground, shut his eyes and walked to Daisy.

"We are in trouble," Kit said as Daisy carried on collecting belongings.

"Why? We survived, we just need to find the princess and we will be fine," Daisy said, putting on a ring she had pulled off a dead man's finger.

"They were sent by Eva, she wants the throne, this is not good." Kit looked at the bracelet shoved into her hand. Kit blinked with dismay. "Daisy, this is serious!" she exclaimed holding the bracelet in her hand not knowing what to do with it.

"Yes, I am aware, but for one moment just be happy we survived, we are okay and let's face it we won't get any thanks from the king. So take the bracelet, we will find the princess and we will sort this out, we always do," she said in a matter of fact tone.

This was exactly why she and Daisy were best friends. She always knew what to do and what to say. Kit smiled at her. "You're right." She let out a sigh. "I think the princess went up the rocky path. We will need to leave the horses down here," Kit said, putting the bracelet on.

"Try to stop worrying so much, Eva won't get the throne, she will be stopped. Our job is the princess's safety," Daisy said with hands on her hip. "Eva has always been different we have always known that, but this is something else." Daisy shook her head.

Kit looked down at her bracelet, a fat raindrop landed on the twisted gold wrapped round her wrist. The wind had stopped, and everything was eerie quiet, no birds singing, no rustling of bushes.

She looked up at the grey sky as more raindrops fell, getting heavier and heavier. As the rain hit the ground, the blood started to be washed away as if all evidence of what had occurred needed to be erased. Her white hair plastering to her head, her wet clothes clung to her body, she had seen three warriors escape with their lives, no doubt to get reinforcements. She let out a sigh as she watched Daisy walk over to the rocky path leading up to the mountains. As she followed, the rain beat down harder still.

"Puzat, wait under the cover of trees, I won't be long," she whispered to him as he followed her to the beginning of the path.

The path was littered with pebbles, jagged stones and heather growing between the cracks. As she walked up the steep incline her foot slipped several times. She could hear Daisy's breaths up ahead which sounded slightly laboured to her.

"You okay up there?" Kit asked.

"Of course, I'm just clearly not as fit as I thought I was," Daisy laughed back at her.

They reached a fork in the path: one leading to the left and one running along the cliff top. Kit bent down to see a piece of heather that had been stood on, she pointed to the cliff top path.

"I think they're close," she informed Daisy, who was still trying to catch her breath.

Daisy raised a finger to her lips as she leant towards the path, listening for sounds of life, as they listened, they could hear slight murmurs.

"Definitely this path, better see if she is okay," Daisy said, continuing over the rocky path.

As they continued on the path near the rocky cliff edge, the sound of the murmuring got louder, the rainfall made the path very slippery underfoot, Daisy slipped several times. The path led to what looked like a wall covered in ivy but they could hear clear voices near to an argument behind it.

Kit frowned. "At least we know she's alive, however she is not being very discreet." Daisy snorted out a laugh, parted the ivy and stood in the alcove.

"Your Majesty," Daisy said with a slight bow of the head. "Please try and be as quiet as possible."

Kit stepped next to her and let the curtain fall back down.

"We need to go, three red warriors fled. They will be back. We have to get away from this place." She looked at Daisy in the dull light.

"To the palace?" the princess asked hopefully.

"Perhaps, your majesty, I do have some bad news to tell you however. It's looking like what happened today has come from the palace." Kit looked down at her hands, the blood from the metal fangs drying into a sharp line.

Before the princess could protest, Daisy said in an even tone, "Eva had them sent to kill you." Kit turned sharply at Daisy, creasing her brow.

The princess let out a little shocked gasp.

Kit cut in, directing her attention to the Mage, "Hello, thank you for saving the princess, it was an incredibly brave thing you did."

Before the Mage could reply, "We must go, Princess, time is very limited they will be back," Daisy urged, turning and opening the ivy curtain.

She reached out and grabbed the hand of the princess and started leading her towards the rocky path.

"Who's your friend?" Daisy asked, looking quizzically as the Mage followed them out.

"She is not my friend, just someone trying to kill my dad," the princess replied noncommittally with a half shrug.

Daisy's head whipped around, staring at the cloaked pauper woman following them, she frowned at the princess.

Chapter Twelve

Eva sat smugly in the room she had hired at the brothel, no one would notice a girl here, and there were always dozens of them which meant she could easily slip in and out. She gazed at herself in her bronze polished mirror, admiring her looks, thinking to herself how easy it was going to be to become the princess. She had been growing her hair out for weeks, no one noticing as she neatly wore it in a tight bun fastened with pins, and she had also started to steal dresses from the princess. Doing it so easily when she had taken them to be cleaned, she had simply slipped them into her chamber room. She giggled to herself. It had all been too easy to be honest. After they were assassinated, she would return in a ripped bedraggled dress with a few minor scrapes so it looked realistic, the medicine lady would say she needs rest, no disturbance until the wedding day and by this point it would be too late for people to stop her. Eva had thought long and hard about the king and Queen who would be the only people to recognise her, but she waved that thought away as she had come to the conclusion that by the time she married and moved into the palace with Prince Geoffrey they wouldn't have to see her. Everyone was going to think she had been killed along with the other ladies in waiting no one would even guess her real identity, especially not Prince Geoffrey as he wouldn't notice one brown-haired girl to another as he never seemed interested in Nekite anyway, but Eva was going to make him interested in her. Her mother had once told her she could be and do anything she wanted to in this life and her only wish was to rule the kingdom, therefore Nekite had to go. She sat in the squalid, dark, damp room with only one candle to light it, reading from waxed papers reciting Celtic words of evil, pictures danced in front of her, the table and barrel shook, she looked every part the witch that she really was.

The rain lashed at their backs as they stumbled down the rocky cliff path towards the track beneath, the procession gingerly took small steps over pebbles, stones and shrubbery, trying to avoid injury. As they reached the bottom the track had turned into a rushing river ankle deep, the force of the water pulling anything small enough away with it down the track. Kit thought it wouldn't be long before the bodies were swept away as the wind whipped around her chilling her to her bone. The horses, which had been pulling the carriage, had disappeared leaving them with no way of getting back to the palace. Kit thought to herself if they didn't move quick the whole path was likely to flood, and judging by how fast the rain was hammering down it wouldn't take long.

"We have to get out of here and quickly," Kit said, once the others had climbed down from the rocky path.

She wiped a strand of wet hair from her face and shouted for Puzat. He came wading across the water towards her resembling a drowned rat.

"Right princess, I'm going to put you on my horse, you will be safe up there and we won't lose you." Kit smiled at the shaken princess.

Kit holstered the princess on to Puzat with ease and turned towards the pauper.

"We haven't been properly introduced, I'm Kit and this is Daisy," she said, pointing in the direction of Daisy who was retrieving Demon.

"We are the princess's guards." She smiled at the pauper. "The kingdom thanks you for what you did today."

The Mage dared to look at Kit for the first time and spoke very quietly, "No need to thank me, I'm known as the Mage."

Kit smiled at her, she could tell she was very nervous of her and Daisy, that didn't surprise her however because who wasn't? Kit had known from the very first moment she had clapped eyes on this girl that she was involved in the revolt, all the soldiers had been talking about them, and the graffiti on walls around the kingdom signifying the rightful king would rule someday. Sometimes a revolt member would be caught and put on trial or even killed. Some of the younger soldiers even feared the revolt but from what she had witnessed today they just looked like paupers with wooden sticks as swords to Kit.

Daisy had successfully retrieved her horse and was dragging her through the torrent of water which had risen to the horse's knees. Rocks had started to crumble from the cliff top from the force of the rain hitting and bouncing off of them. The sky was such a dark grey it was almost black with heavy clouds circling.

Daisy struggled over to the carriage to gather some of the princess's belongings which she slung over her horse.

"I am ready," Daisy shouted into the wind and rain.

The Mage made a decision to follow the gods as she couldn't see any revolt members. None of them had waited for her, she sighed heavily, she hoped they hadn't all been slain here today.

Kit nodded at Daisy and headed up the track, which led towards the palace, they had got no more than half a mile up the track when the water levels had risen to their waist.

As they stopped at a T-junction in the track, Daisy said, "We can't go any further, it's too dangerous."

Kit nodded with a small shiver. She had begun to get cold, her skin looking translucent as they stood discussing what to do next.

"I know where to go," the Mage shouted from the back, clinging on to Puzat's tail. Daisy raised her eyebrows to Kit who simply shrugged back.

"Is it far?" Daisy asked as a floating branch nearly took her off her feet.

"In the woods there's shelter for us all," the Mage replied.

"Lead the way," Daisy said, regaining her balance.

The Mage clung to Puzat for support as she walked ahead, directing them into the forest deeper and deeper. The light grew even darker; the ground sodden and muddy, leaves that had been hammered by the rain fell to the floor. The Mage raised her palm to the tree tops signalling peace to the prying eyes who were all watching with fascination.

"Well, this isn't too creepy," Daisy said through gritted teeth.

"I hope we're not walking into a trap," Kit whispered. Instinctively, her claws protruded through her skin.

After walking all night, they reached a wooden shack which looked like it was falling down, with its shanty roof crooked at an almost jaunty angle. Daisy raised another eyebrow at Kit shaking her head in disbelief.

"Wait here, I will knock," the Mage stated, walking towards the door and giving a big knock. There was no reply.

She knocked again. Still no reply.

"I don't know why they are not opening," she said with a nervous stutter.

Daisy walked forward, gave a big sharp kick, and the door groaned from the pressure. She gave a sigh and kicked harder, which resulted in the door giving way and falling from its hinges. The sound echoed around them.

"Just needed persuading." She smirked at Kit who laughed at her.

The Mage rushed in, scanning the room, everywhere was dark and cold. The fire was stone cold, meaning no one had been here for a while.

The Mage looked wild eyed and close to tears, she collapsed in an exhausted heap on the floor, as Daisy helped the princess in and got her settled on a barrel. Kit had started a fire by creating a spark from rubbing her claws together.

Afterwards, Kit sat on the floor next to the Mage who was muttering over and over to herself.

"Hey shush it's going to be okay, look I've found a note from a man called Alston."

The Mage looked up quickly and gazed at the ragged piece of parchment in Kit's hand, her claws were still protruded, which made the mage recoil slightly. The Mage read through the note several times just to make sure she hadn't misread anything.

In a shaking voice the Mage said, "They're not all dead, thank the gods." She smiled at kit.

The note read:

Dear Mage,

I am alive; however, we have decided to evacuate. We lost

great numbers. The leader has said we will be blamed for what transpired. Better to disappear for a while. Please find us where the river meets the mountains and birds sing their loudest.

Kit smiled back in the dim light from the fire, the shadows danced wildly around them with the warmth enveloping them all.

Kit turned to Daisy. "We shall rest here tonight then make a move at dawn."

"Where are we going to go?" Daisy said, moving closer to the fire.

"Not sure, as we don't know who we can trust at the moment," Kit replied, scratching her head. Daisy sighed deeply.

"Our last mission turns into a right mess." Daisy shook her head staring into the fire.

The Mage looked up. "This was never going to be your last mission; the king was going to stop that. You're just too valuable to him."

Chapter Thirteen

Destin trudged behind the procession of men up a track, carrying his fur bag over his right shoulder, the rain lashed down on him making him involuntarily shudder every now and then. The map of the kingdom they had acquired from the small village on the outskirts of the palace showed a road leading north to the kingdom through what looked to be a treacherous track known as creek's pass. It was the quickest and most direct route to the palace but with plenty of hideouts for thieves and bandits. The track which they trekked on was beginning to flood with water, becoming very slippery underfoot, their leather boots sodden to the woollen sock beneath.

"Is there an alternative route?" Destin shouted from behind, barely audible through the wind and rain.

"Through the forest? Or turn around and go west, then north? Those are the options I can see." Bjoarn turned around squinting at the map which was disintegrating before him.

Neither of them sounded appealing to Destin. They had been walking for almost a day towards this track, if they were to turn round and go west it would be towards the mountain region of the kingdom resulting in many more days of travel, but before Destin could voice his opinion, Bjoarn spoke up.

"We carry on up this path," Bjoarn said, turning to seek approval from the king.

They all carried on trekking up the path, the rain never letting up, and the water rising and rising around them. The rain was beginning to get so heavy that branches were falling from trees which lined the path sides, these branches being swept along with the current of water. The men struggled on for another hour with fruitless results until the king halted with perspiration and water running down his face and turned to face them with a grim look on his face.

"I am afraid we shall have to retrace our steps and head west towards higher ground." He started wading through the water past the men.

They all turned and started off down the track, retracing their steps through the water, huddling together following their king. Destin glanced at the sky as the rain continued to hammer into him, and he had never seen such dark clouds. As he carried on walking, he heard a sharp scream far off into the distance which made him stop in his tracks, he glanced back towards the creek pass. The wind rushed through the trees with the sound of the rain blocking out almost all noise. He shook his head with disbelief. He couldn't have heard anything, maybe this land really was making him crazy.

As the men reached higher ground, they faced a stone with etched markings barely visible through the wear of the ages, Bjoarn wiped the stone to reveal an arrow pointing west and a town name, Montar.

"We shall carry on with our journey until we reach a suitable place to camp for the night," the king informed the bedraggled men. "This town, Montar, must have smaller villages nearby."

The men dutifully nodded and started to follow the king along the track.

They had all slept fitfully that night, Daisy and Kit taking it in turns to be on watch. As the princess drifted in and out of sleep she had dreamt of the faces of her most trusted friends as they met their demise. Every time she woke, she thought it was all just a dream, but as her eyes adjusted to the dark, she saw the near pitch-black shanty like wooden ceiling staring back at her. She had never been in a place like this, on an itchy straw mattress in the damp with others laying right beside her. To Nekite it was like a whole new world compared to the riches, the silk and the comfort that she was used to. At home in the palace, she would be in her huge bed with its richly embroidered canopy with their family's coats of arms suspended from the ceiling with the large headboard protecting her head from the cold hard stone wall. As she lay shivering under the hemp sack she was using as a blanket for warmth she began to silently cry fat warm tears. She let them run down her face.

The Mage pretended that she was asleep, but in reality, she was staring blankly at the wooden wall. In her corner of the room on her usual straw mattress, she too shed silent tears, she couldn't believe that the remaining revolt members hadn't waited for her. She knew she hadn't been long behind them. She shook her head slightly, did they not care for her as much as she cared for them? She had seen many of her friends, people she had considered family, that had been cut down by the sword, way before their time. She felt they should go back, retrieve the bodies, give them a burial so they weren't forgotten. Did the revolt even care if she had died? The doubts swam in front of her eyes round and round in her head. Her brain couldn't process the turn of events which had happened, but a small part of her realised she had in fact achieved the mission as she was travelling with the gods and not only that but she had saved the princess's life. In a small way she felt proud.

Kit and Daisy were sitting closer to the door as the sun started to rise. Daisy stirred awake, she rubbed her eyes with her fist and blinked a couple of times, adjusting to her surroundings. She slowly sat up and saw Kit leant against the door frame with a candle nearly burnt down to the wick.

"Rise and shine," Kit said with laughter in her voice.

"I have such a sore neck, not the comfiest of places to sleep," Daisy said, trying to stretch her neck out.

"No, it's not great, but at least we had a roof over our heads, the forest looked spooky." Kit smiled and chuckled to herself.

"Yes, having to have a peace sign on your hand to pass through, no wonder soldiers always went round it," Daisy said rubbing her neck and shoulder.

"I don't suppose you have had any bright ideas regarding getting back into the palace or what to do next." Kit looked at Daisy with exhausted-looking eyes.

"I'm afraid not, I hoped you would." Daisy laughed back at her.

Kit pulled her cloak around her body. "I believe the Mage regarding us not being free; I had thought it was too good to be true."

Daisy sighed with discontent. "I agree that we are too powerful to let go, who else would defeat twelve devils on horseback." She raised her eyebrows questioningly.

Kit smiled at this but paused for a few moments, lost in thought.

"I don't want to return." Kit pulled her legs to her body and rocked slightly to and fro.

"When you do that, you look like you have gone insane, sat in an asylum." Daisy laughed with a raised eyebrow.

"Probably where I will end up." Kit laughed back.

"Do you really believe that we are not free woman then?" Daisy asked, suddenly looking serious.

Kit sighed. "Unfortunately, I think she speaks the truth, we win so many battles I suspect it is unlikely we are free as we have well known powerful magic, which is forbidden." Kit turned to look at Daisy who had started to stand up and gather belongings.

"I fear you are right, I suppose they will kill us before letting us retire, we have only done the minimal soldier service, in the king's eyes we could go on for years more as we are still young," Daisy said closing her hemp bag.

"I do not think I could go on for years, I hate it there. I have been wishing for my freedom for far too long." Kit also started to gather her belongings.

They carried on in silence for a few seconds, both mulling over the actions that were needed next. Daisy broke the silence first.

"Ok so the plan." She paused, looking Kit in the eyes. "People think we are both dead right?" Daisy said suddenly less serious and smiley.

Kit frowned at her in amusement. "Yes." She drew out the words slowly.

"Therefore, it is simple. We shall remain dead, the princess will return but we won't," Daisy said, beaming.

Kit nodded and scratched her chin. "That actually might work, we will have to make sure the princess returns safely though."

"Naturally," Daisy said, going to wake the others up. Kit watched Daisy crawl over to the others with a smile on her face, the idea wasn't half bad and maybe, just maybe, they could pull it off, she might get her freedom.

Daisy shook the Mage, who had finally fallen asleep, awake. The Mage opened her eyes slowly to find purple hair in her face; she rubbed the sleep out of her eyes.

Daisy smiled down at her. "Wakey, wakey, sleepy head."

The Mage grunted and her tummy rumbled. She couldn't remember when she had last eaten. She rolled off her straw mattress and went towards the pantry at the back of the wooden shack in search of anything edible.

"Princess, we need to start to move on soon," Daisy gently whispered.

Nekite stirred, sleeping on the hard straw mattress had made her back sore and itchy. Daisy held out a hand for her to help the princess up.

The Mage returned with crusty-looking bread and some apples which were on the turn. The princess looked at the morsels of food with disgust but took them regardless. Her stomach felt like it was doing flips, she was that hungry. As she gingerly took a bite of the bread it felt like her teeth would snap off it was that hard. Nekite looked over at the Mage eagerly tucking into the bread without hesitation whilst collecting more possessions she was putting in a hessian moth-eaten bag.

"How do you live like this?" the princess blurted out, still trying to chew on the rock-like bread.

The Mage suddenly looked up at the princess, then at her surroundings: the dark room, the cobwebs, the mismatched furniture, if one could call it furniture, the damp seeping in through the shanty windows and the smell of the forest.

"Believe it or not this is nice compared to some places I've lived." She laughed and carried on sorting through her limited belongings.

Nekite looked at her in surprise. "You are joking with me, aren't you?" She looked quizzically at the Mage.

The Mage shook her head and laughed.

Eva was in the process of cutting the dress she had stolen from the princess when she had a knock on the door. She looked up quizzically; no one knew she was here so it was indeed very strange for someone to be at her door.

She grabbed a dagger from the bedside table, walking slowly to the door she hesitantly spoke, "Hello who is there?"

"Your lady, it is I, general of the red coats," the man spoke with urgency in his voice.

Eva's brows furrowed slightly, anxiety building up within her as she opened the door so a sliver of light flooded through to the room.

The red devil stood in front of her, clearly injured, and slightly shook up but trying to appear the fearless warrior she had entrusted to kill the princess and guards.

"Please, come in I don't want anyone overhcaring us." Eva looked down the dimly-lit corridor to make sure no one was around.

She let the warrior general in first and followed with her dagger behind her back, just in case she needed it. She watched him glance around the room and she nodded towards the bed indicating he could take a seat there.

"Your lady, the task failed." But before he could finish his sentence she interrupted with a sharp: "Excuse me what does that mean it failed?"

But before he could answer she said in a harsh low tone, "You are supposed to be the best."

"Your lady, we are the best but we were against gods with claws as hands and fangs hanging from their mouth, we simply stood no chance," he replied with head hung low.

"How many survived?" she asked, starting to pace the small room.

"No one survived apart from the gods, the princess and a pauper," he said, still looking at the floor.

"A pauper you say? That's interesting, no ladies and no guards?" Eva asked still pacing but slowing down.

He simply shook his head.

"This might not be such a big problem in that case," Eva muttered to herself.

"Okay so the only real setback is the princess." She carried on pacing, talking to herself. "The gods could become the scapegoat," she mused to herself.

The red warrior just sat in silence just watching her pace around the room muttering to herself.

"How much money does it take for you and your men to find and kill the princess?" She stopped, looked straight at the man sat on the bed, and smiled sweetly.

"What about the gods? Only three of us escaped, they are very powerful I would need a whole set of new men." His head hung low again as he stared at the floor.

"I will pay you well for your troubles and a bonus for the death of the princess," she replied, the dagger still in her hand.

The warrior general looked at her in astonishment. She knew he could not refuse this offer. "Yes, your lady I will round up more men." He stood to leave.

"She can't survive," Eva said, tilting her head to the right.

The red General left swiftly through the door and down the dim corridor without making a noise.

Eva settled herself back on the bed, this was an inconvenience, but it was still going to work. She had too much riding on this.

Chapter Fourteen

Kit, Daisy, the Mage and the princess all set out from the revolt's hideout once everyone had eaten and gathered anything they might need. They headed towards the mountain region of the kingdom which was west of the track on which so many had been killed yesterday. The rain had stopped overnight leaving a damp smell in the air, Kit led Puzat with the princess sat on top so she didn't get harmed in any way whilst everyone's bags were placed upon Demon. They trudged through the forest, following every step the Mage made, trying not to stumble over fallen branches, or slip on sodden leaves. After what seemed like hours of walking, they reached a clearing where they stopped. Kit helped the princess off of Puzat. The princess tried to stretch her legs but as she did so an arrow shot down, narrowly missing her foot.

"Get down princess," Kit shouted, running over to her with a shield raised against any more arrows.

Kit's claws shot out of her hand, whilst Daisy's fangs fell from her mouth. They let out a primeval animal-like noise as they stared up at the trees above and chanting noises surrounded them. The Mage stared at them with awe, she couldn't take her eyes away from them, an arrow whistled past her which broke the trance. She walked over to where they were stood with her hand raised high showing the etched eye symbol. The arrows and chanting suddenly stopped. Kit and

Daisy both looked at her in surprise as the Mage started speaking in tongues towards the trees.

"Well, it gets weirder," Daisy whispered in Kit's ear.

Before Kit could reply, a blue-bodied muscular man dropped out of the trees, covered only in long dark wavy hair down to his shoulders and a scrap of fur covering his modesty. Daisy's eyes were out on stalks watching the man walk towards the Mage still talking their own language.

"I think I like weird," Daisy said, still not taking her eyes away from him.

Kit couldn't help but laugh at her, the princess who was cowering behind a shield stood and hid behind Kit, peeping round to get a look at what was happening.

The Mage turned to them. "This is Murgo, the son of the king of the Celts, but you would know them by the name savages."

Daisy smiled at him. "Hi," she said in a little girl voice.

"Jeez," Kit spluttered, rolling her eyes.

"What is she doing?" Nekite whispered to Kit.

"This is just what Daisy is like, needing male attention most of the time. You will get used to it." Kit laughed as the princess just frowned.

Daisy couldn't stop looking at the Celtic warrior as the Mage walked away from the man towards where they all stood, staring in shock and amazement at what was happening.

"Nothing to fear, I have spoken to Murgo he said he and his men will accompany us safely across the forest," the Mage stated.

Kit looked over towards the Celtic people trying to gauge if this was a safe idea, as moments before they had just nearly shot them with arrows. As she stood staring without blinking, she took in the different blue patterns across the men's bodies, some with tribal words written as protection. She had never seen anything like it before. The Mage coughed slightly which brought Kit back to the huddled group.

"Can we trust him?" Kit asked, looking over the Mage's shoulders again at the blue men.

"Yes, they are peaceful people who believe in the magic of the land, we have nothing to fear as we are not threatening their existence," the Mage replied, turning to Murgo. "Lead the way." The Mage smiled at him.

Daisy was smiling to herself and muttered, "This just gets better and better."

Kit looked at her and chuckled to herself. They followed his lead, winding around trees. His men followed behind and in the tree tops, jumping from one branch to another.

The grace that these so-called savages had amazed Kit, as they swung from the trees with so little effort whilst making no noise at all, it was no wonder they could ambush people. The princess had dismounted Puzat, giving his back a rest. She walked behind Kit, following her every move. They carried on through the forest for another two hours until the sun had begun to go down and the dim light played with their eyes.

"We shall call it a day," Murgo said in broken English.

"I love the accent, wonder if he's married," Daisy said to Kit, getting their sacks from Demon.

"Ask him, you have never been shy before." Kit laughed.

"Ok I will." Daisy flicked her hair and marched over to where he was stood with his men chatting in their own tongue.

Kit watched her with sheer amazement. Nothing stopped that girl, not even an attempted assassination. She turned to tend to Puzat, who the princess was gingerly holding, keeping her feet encased in embroidered satin shoes well away from his hooves.

"It would appear you have never held a horse before." Kit smiled and took the reins from her, as she took the saddle off and placed it on the floor propped up against a tree.

The princess replied, "Not really, I have always had servants to do that for me, in fact I haven't really done much on my own." She looked at the floor.

Kit glanced at her, with her soft skin and pale complexion, it didn't surprise Kit at all that the princess was this way.

"I see, well, whilst we are here on this journey there will be lots of opportunity for you to experience life slightly more." Kit smiled at her and patted Puzat, tethering him to a nearby tree.

The Mage appeared next to Nekite making her jump. "Sorry, your majesty, I did not mean to startle you, Murgo's men are hunting our dinner as we speak, we shall have a feast tonight." The Mage smiled and patted her stomach.

"It is against the law to hunt the king's animals," Nekite furrowed her brow.

The Mage laughed. "The king has no power over the forests, he and the rest of the kingdom are scared of them. You will come to understand that."

The Mage walked away towards the men who were making the fire for whatever animal they could find.

"My father is not a well-liked man, is he?" the princess asked, quietly watching the mage walk away.

Kit tilted her head to the right slightly and thought carefully about what to say.

"No princess he isn't, I am not fond of him myself. Have you been to the slums of the city walls? Have you seen how people are living? I am sorry to inform you your father is a greedy man taking land and kingdoms but not providing for the people who live there." Kit sighed. "He is also a liar, he informed me and Daisy we are free after ten years' service which we have served with honour, but I have been told he has gone back on his word, meaning we will have to carry on fighting in his name. Not something I am prepared to do."

Nekite stared at Kit for a second, processing what she had just heard. "I am sorry he has done this to you and to the people of the kingdom. I hope to rectify this when I have more power."

Kit started to walk towards the warmth of the fire with the princess stumbling behind her. "I am sorry to tell you this, your majesty, but your marriage to Prince Geoffrey stops you having any control over the kingdom until your father dies, you will simply go to Carak and produce heirs." Kit shrugged her shoulders.

The princess stopped dead in her tracks trying to process what she had just heard. She didn't want to believe it but something inside of her was telling her it was true.

Destin woke with a start. Sweat dripped from his forehead, his eyes wide with fright, his heart hammering in his chest. As the vivid dream of battle and blood loss faded into the dusky morning, he told himself it had all been a nightmare and nothing to worry about. He turned to see his brothers all asleep around the dying fire. They had set camp up inside a deserted and run-down village which had been known as Billred, sleeping in the long-forgotten huts which made up the village. The sun was just starting to rise, casting everything into dark long shadows. As Destin sat for a moment lost in thought, the faint sound of galloping horses could just be heard, the sound grew louder bringing him out of his trance. His brothers hadn't woken so he grabbed his sword and crawled to the door, which was leant heavily to one side as the top hinge had rusted away. Through a crack in the door, he could just see three red devils riding solid black horses race through the long-forgotten village, solid clumps of mud flying in the air as the horses tore up the overgrown land. Destin had never seen anything like this with his own eyes. His heart hammering, he leant his forehead on the rotting door and sighed with relief.

"What is this place?" he asked himself in a hushed whispered voice.

"Brother are you okay?" Bjoarn sat up and rubbed his eyes wearily.

"You wouldn't believe me if I told you," Destin laughed to his brother. "I'm sure my eyes are playing tricks on me."

"Did you see another ghostly blue man?" Bjoarn laughed and crawled over to the door.

"No just three red devils riding horses." Destin shrugged his shoulders and glanced through the crack again.

Bjoarn looked quizzically at him. "Yes, you have gone mad." He clapped him on the back.

Before Destin could speak, Bjoarn stated, "I think you need the company of a good woman." He laughed to himself. "We shall move on tonight, find a town, and have some fun."

Destin didn't respond. He turned and looked out of the crack in the door half expecting to see the devils coming back. He knew what he had seen was real. He shook his head slightly trying to forget.

When night fell, the lights of the town upon the hill shown bright compared to the dark night sky, Destin stared up at it excitement flowing through him. They had been raiding for many weeks now, therefore a break was well overdue. He could tell that his brother Bjoarn was very excited at the chance to let his hair down. As the men entered the town, they split off into smaller groups. Destin entered a tavern with Bjoarn and Ethan. The noise of chatter engulfed them; they had to jostle towards the bar to get a tankard of mead.

Once they had received their drinks, Destin took in their surroundings, candle light gave a warm glow, boar heads adorned the walls. Coats of arms hung from the rafters which nearly hit Destin's tall head. They huddled in the corner sipping on their drinks, Bjoarn had already seen a woman he liked the look of, his attention completely diverted on her. She was busty with a solid metal clasp under her bosom giving the effect of lifting them to the sky. She was wiggling her hips proactively towards the three men in the corner, however Destin had no desire for that tonight. He kept glancing out the window at the rising fog, noticing every time he looked out different shapes rising and falling in the mist spooking him more then he would like to admit. He took a sip of his mead to calm his nerves, he shook his head slightly, this was proving to be a very different raid to the others they had taken part in: no slaves so far were taken just jewels and riches. Destin did begin to wonder if it was really worth it.

"After tonight we are heading for the kingdom, this is our last stop," Bjoarn cut into Destin's thoughts.

"I am aware," Destin replied, shifting on the barrel he was sitting on.

"I'm meaning to have some fun, look at Ethan he can't get enough of it here." Bjoarn nodded with laughter to where their younger brother was merrily dancing with several local girls.

Destin sighed heavily, turning towards the window, losing himself to his thoughts once again.

Chapter Fifteen

Butterflies started swarming inside Daisy's stomach as she approached the blue men around the fire; she mentally shook herself and told herself to get a grip. She smiled widely as she stood and cleared her throat to get Murgo's attention. At the sound of the noise, he turned and looked at her and returned the smile.

"Hello, I am not sure the Mage has introduced us." She smiled sweetly at him.

"She mentioned the names of her travelling companions, but not exactly who is who." He stood up and faced her, guiding her gently to the side away from his men.

"Well in that case I am Daisy, I am one of the princess's guards," she said, following him.

He nodded and said, "The Mage said you were gods." He paused, regarding her. "But the gods I know of don't walk on this earth. I have heard others say you are monsters. I know they walk this earth." He looked at her sceptically, taking a step away from her.

She gave a small sad smile, looked at Kit talking to the Mage, and realised at once why Kit never tried with men, why she never put herself out there. With a small shake of the head Daisy knew Kit was right, no one understood them.

She looked at Murgo, her mouth smiled but her eyes did not. "We are no gods or monsters just very broken people."

With that she turned and walked with purpose towards Kit. Kit enveloped her into a hug instantly without questioning her. The princess watched them interact and got a pang of jealousy flaring up within her for the two friends; in her entire life she had never had real true friends like her guards who she was certain would lay their lives on the line for each other.

Kit wiped the tears from Daisy's face as Daisy said, "I don't want to be different any more." She buried her head into Kit's shoulder.

"I know, sweetie, it really is not fair, but just think what we have accomplished, how far we have come. We are not even supposed to be here in this time, in this era. We didn't die that day, we flourished." Kit stared at Daisy, smiling at her. Daisy nodded back.

Daisy snuffled. "You are right it just doesn't get easier." She stared at the floor for a moment. "I'm okay now, just had to get that off my chest." She smiled at Kit, releasing the hug.

Murgo was still stood staring at them, with a frown painted on his face, thinking to himself they certainly did not act like monsters.

That night after food, the Celtic men sung whilst the Mage danced around the glowing fire. She had even made the princess join in when possible. Nekite was laughing so much her face had begun to hurt.

Kit sat and smiled in their direction but her mind was far away in a time long gone, a time when they had just arrived on this land, a time where gods were created. She was remembering falling, the never-ending uncontrollable feeling of falling. She remembered the ground appearing quickly, getting closer and closer, the feeling of hitting branch after branch until nothing but black.

The day after their escape from the laboratory was etched in their minds. On that day Kit stirred from her position sprawled on the ground, she could faintly hear rushing water crashing over rocks, the sun so bright and warming on the skin, she couldn't remember when she had last felt the sun on her skin. She raised her head, slightly wincing as she did so, her neck stiff from lying in an awkward position, her eyes focused on the dappled sunlight that filtered through the leafy coverage of trees and the birds singing, flying from one tree to another. She gulped down breaths of clean fresh air.

"Daisy," she hoarsely whispered.

There was no response, just silence. A rise of panic seared through her. "Daisy where are you?" Kit tried again, this time louder.

She slowly sat up, her neck throbbing as she did so. Rubbing it distractedly, she looked at her surroundings with utter shock. Wherever she was, it definitely was not the laboratory. As she tried to stand, she collapsed, her legs giving way instantly, she felt like she had no strength left in her body. She went on to her hands and knees trying to push herself up, falling down again. Her ankles were aching, her knees were stiff, she was worried she had seriously injured herself during the fall. Kit crawled over to a tree, propping herself against it.

After around an hour of Kit drifting in and out of consciousness she heard.

"Kit, I'm over here," Daisy hoarsely shouted over to where Kit had rested.

Kit looked round searching for the voice. She crawled on her hands and knees around a huge oak tree trying not to put pressure on her ankle, and it was there that she saw Daisy all dishevelled propped up against another enormous tree. Kit smiled from ear to ear.

Kit sighed with relief at the sight of her friend, "are you okay?" she asked catching her breath.

Daisy nodded back at her. "Yeah, I'm just very sore, what happened to us? It was the strangest thing, so surreal, so many lights," Daisy said, clutching her head.

Kit agreed, "We are definitely not in the laboratory any more." She giggled with a mixture of excitement and nerves.

Daisy crawled on her hands and knees to where Kit was kneeled on the floor, drawing her into a tight hug. As they let go of each other, Daisy looked around taking in the beautiful scenery of the flowing river, the magnificent trees and the dappled sunlight.

Daisy suddenly exclaimed, "We did it, we escaped, I almost cannot believe it." She let out a squeal of excitement.

Kit laughed at her reaction but could feel the excitement in the pit of her stomach almost making her giddy. However, a cautious feeling also mingled into her emotions.

"We need to find out where we are and how we got here," Daisy said, standing up hesitantly.

As Kit followed suit and gingerly stood up her ankle throbbed, she ripped part of the laboratory gown she wore and wrapped it tightly round the ankle in the hope this would support it enough until they found help. They both decided to walk through the wooded area in which they had landed. They walked for hours and hours, their feet blistered, sore and swollen but they never stopped walking. Kit couldn't believe the beauty of the land, it was so different to the four walls of the cell she had lived in for so many years, even her home land didn't compare to this. Their journey took them up a rocky coastal path alongside a steep cliff in which you could see for miles and miles. To Kit and Daisy, who had never seen the sea before, their excitement was barely containable. The waves crashed against the viscous-looking rocks beneath causing white spray which mesmerized the girls, the seagulls squawking overhead gliding in and out of the sea effortlessly.

Even though both Kit and Daisy had no idea where they were heading, or even in which country they were standing, they both felt safe and could taste the freedom they had so often sought after. In the dead of night, they hunted animals such as rabbits, hares and birds which they ate next to the warmth of small fires glowing dimly in the dark. With every mile they walked, Kit became increasingly aware that neither of them had seen any sign of human life, no houses, no cars, no planes, no sign of any modern life crossed their path. After many days walking through fields, wooded areas, across streams, up cliffs and down hills they reached a tall sturdy rock embedded in the ground. Etched in the rock was the word Belware.

Kit stared at the stone with furrowed brows. "Belware? Hmm, not heard of it, have you? The stone doesn't help much," Kit said chewing her lip with concentration. "A map would be great right about now," she continued, scratching her head.

Daisy looked at the stone with puzzlement, turning to Kit she said, "I can't say I've ever heard of a place with such a name before, but we might as well follow this direction. Who knows, we might actually be getting somewhere now."

Kit followed Daisy's direction, tripping up over the rutted muddy ground which looked like it was supposed to be a type of road. Kit thought to herself how rural the track looked without the use of tarmac or cement which the girls were both used to. The sun had begun to set, leaving threatening shadows in its wake, the sound of crows filled the air as the first heavy rain drop hit the ground, soaking it through, as the heavens opened and rain poured down. Kit looked at Daisy, as they rushed under the cover of the nearby trees, she was shaking slightly. Kit enveloped her in a hug and in an aid to share body heat. They had just decided that staying there for the night in such weather would be for the best when Kit noticed something large and dark hanging from a tree further up on the other side of the track.

As she squinted her eyes to get a better look, she tapped Daisy on the shoulder. "I'm going to investigate that." She pointed to the shape in the trees.

Daisy eyes widened. "Please be careful, it could be anything, maybe just leave it." Her voice was unsure.

Kit smiled at Daisy and reassuringly said, "Don't worry you can see me and I won't be long."

Kit kept her head down against the rain and stepped onto the track which had turned into a sloppy, mucky mess. She slipped about trying to reach the tree which was a few meters up from where the girls were sheltering from the rain. As soon as Kit got nearer, she didn't have to leave the track to know what the dark shape hanging in the trees was. She turned around quickly and made her way back to Daisy without falling over.

"So what is it?" Daisy asked, her arms folded over her chest trying to keep warm.

"I don't think we should stay here tonight," is all Kit could manage.

"But why? The weather is awful and I'm tired. No, actually not just tired, I am exhausted," Daisy replied, sounding stroppy.

"That shape," Kit said, pointing in the direction of the tree, "is a dead person obviously hung for whatever reason."

For a second Daisy couldn't reply due to shock. "Are you serious! What do we do?"

Kit just shook her head, close to tears with exhaustion and fear as the realization of not knowing what was happening to them hit her like a ton of bricks. She tried to speak but her throat was choked with tears.

Daisy was staring at the person swaying slightly left and right in the wind and rain when she suddenly said, "At least we have seen another human. I was beginning to panic we were the only ones." She then let out a nervous giggle.

Kit looked at Daisy, blinking back the tears, she managed to laugh back. "I was beginning to think that as well."

Both Kit and Daisy had decided to keep trekking on the path instead of sheltering under the tree, taking the deceased person as a warning, they hurried along the slippery path. After half an hour of struggling against the elements they rounded a corner to be awestruck by a huge stone castle protected by a wall in the distance. Even in the rain and wind the castle stood out like a beacon. It was huge, the biggest building either Kit or Daisy had seen. With every step towards the castle Kit started to see signs of human life, small pens which housed sheep and goats grazing happily along the road side. Attached to them were wooden shack-like houses with smoke billowing from the centre chimney. There were piles of rubbish in buckets assaulting their sense of smell on every corner and the track became more and more worn with the wheels of carts pulled either by oxen or horse.

The sound of people talking, laughing and shouting filled

their ears, it was almost like music to Kit, who had feared for their safety. They entered the main gates to the city to see peasant children playing by the moat-like river covered in mud and grime, some missing teeth as they gave a gappy smile. People bustled past the two shocked soaked girls, some shoving them out of the way with their laden carts, chickens; goat's, horses and cows all adding to the choir of noise that filled the air.

Daisy pulled herself together and walked over to the market place which was in full swing. She grabbed the attention of a butcher who was busy chopping huge chunks of pig legs up.

"Hello, sir, I am just enquiring about the time, date and the city name please?" she said with a smile.

The portly man covered in blood looked quizzically at Daisy and replied, "The date is May the twenty-second of the year 900 AD in the city of Belware.

Chapter Sixteen

Daisy was huddled next to Kit with the princess the other side just a few feet from the dying embers of the fire, when Puzat nudged Kit out of her deep thoughts. She glanced up to see the darkness had enveloped them. She turned her head to see that Murgo was crouched chatting to his friends near the trees the other side of the fire. He had that authoritative aura which glowed, surrounding him, which made most people trust him, however Kit found she felt uneasy and not able to do so and definitely not his men. She knew this needed to change if he were to carry on being their travelling companion, but she couldn't see anything bad happen to Daisy and the princess. She raised her eyebrows. She knew from this moment that the Mage was now one of them, meaning she wouldn't let anything happen to her either. Kit let out a long sigh. She wiggled her way out of where she had been resting, stood up with a stretch and gracefully walked towards the men. They had not heard her, she was careful with every step she took. She had reached a nearby tree which she was compelled to hide behind to listen to the voices with their manly tones. Kit furrowed her brows, the blue men spoke their native tongue which she didn't understand. Under her breath she muttered a string of ancient words, the wind suddenly picked up, stirring the fallen leaves around her feet. The trees swayed right and left as if dancing to the words she had just muttered. Then as soon as the wind started it stopped and once again everything was quite apart from the men speaking; now every word spoken she could fully understand.

"We should leave them here, they are not our people, they will bring bad fortune upon our clan," a man with a blue torso addressed Murgo.

"I have made a promise to the Mage to guide them through the forest," Murgo said with ease and a slight shrug of his shoulder to his men, signifying his decision was final.

"If I may speak so boldly, I think that is poor judgment on your part, it is only the purple-haired woman that has turned your head," the man replied to Murgo in a harsh voice.

Kit raised her eyebrow, so he did like Daisy, she smiled slightly at the thought but before he could reply the man carried on speaking in a hushed whisper.

"I am certain they are devils, no gods look, or act like that, not in the stories I have been told!" he exclaimed.

With little thought, Murgo replied, "That is what I first thought, but they have saved the princess, kept the Mage alive and even comforted one another. That is not the behaviour of devils, I know devils are wicked evil beings that solely live to cause havoc and unhappiness, these individuals are no such things," he said with conviction.

The men all grunted, looked around to see if they had been heard, then carried on with their conversation.

Kit smiled slightly, before making her way back, silently and stealthily, to where Daisy and the princess were sleeping under the watch of Puzat.

Daisy had woken with a start, her heart pounding, sweat ran off her head in little droplets. She looked around at the unfamiliar scenery: the woodland, the bird's squawking. She lifted her hands up to shield her eyes from the stark sunlight blazing through the tree branches. It took her a moment to remember what had happened and why they were here, she turned to see Kit looking at her with a frown plastered over her face.

"Are you okay? You look like you have seen a ghost." Kit rubbed her eyes sleepily.

"Yes, I am fine, I just woke up all disorientated, I have a bad feeling." She sighed. "I am probably just tired." She smiled at Kit.

"Yes, not the most comfortable sleep I have ever had." Kit rubbed her eyes and looked at down at the princess who was wrapped under Puzat's saddle blanket.

The Mage blinked her eyes open at the sound of them chatting, took in her surroundings and sighed heavily. She was still hurting over the revolt members choice to leave her behind. She wanted them to be proud of her. She had succeeded. She was with the gods, she was travelling with them, helping them. She had even slept next to them, felt their body heat, but her family, as she saw them, had left her. Anger built up within her, even the gods had comforted her for the brief moment the despair threatened to swallow her. She sat up as Kit asked.

"Are you all right? How did you sleep?" She smiled easily at her.

The Mage sniffled, on the verge of tears, she couldn't get the thought out of her head that she may never see her family again, her dreams that night had been filled with such thoughts. A tear slid down her check.

Kit moved over and hugged her tightly. When she stopped, she smiled and said, "We just have to help each other that is all we can do for now."

The Mage nodded in response.

Murgo's men prepared a quick breakfast of leftover meat which Kit and Daisy found hard to stomach so early on in the day. After they had all eaten, they carried on with their journey through the endless stream of trees and woodland area. The princess had grown tired from the reality of what had happened, exhaustion and the hard truths about her father. She sat numbly aboard Puzat, being lifted on and off when he needed a break. She silently followed Daisy without as much as a blink. Daisy started to worry that the princess had completely lost her mind and kept whispering to Kit that they needed to do something to jolt her out of it.

After they had walked all night, they reached the edge of the forest. Murgo instructed they should stay here for the night then start the mountain climb at dawn when everyone was well rested and refreshed which made Kit snort with laughter. It was going to take more than a night for her to feel anywhere near refreshed.

Daisy nudged her as if to say stop being rude whilst she lifted the princess off of Puzat for the last time that day.

"Hey, Princess are you all right, you have been very quiet today?" Daisy asked, sitting her down on the saddle blanket.

The princess didn't look up to acknowledge she had heard the question. She simply carried on with a vague expression written on her face staring into space. The Mage glanced at Daisy and pulled a face which Daisy assumed mirrored her own expression of confusion mixed with worry. But they didn't have time to worry as Murgo's men, who had gone on the hunt for food, came crashing back through the branches shouting and pointing wildly in all directions.

Kit came to stand with Daisy and the Mage, their metal claws and fangs instinctively extracting to full length. The Mage, who was standing in between them, took in the sight of the breathtaking metal claws belonging to Kit and the huge fangs past Daisy's chin. She suddenly felt a sensation she had rarely felt before; complete safety.

Murgo ordered his men to check on the noise which was heading along the track a few feet from their hidden position in the forest.

"Were your men seen?" Daisy asked in a hushed whisper as Murgo stood with them with his weapon drawn.

"I am unable to say for sure," he replied with wide eyes as his men's shouts increased to frenzy then suddenly went deathly silent.

A glimpse of red flashed through the trees, no birds made a sound, no tree rustled its leaves, just the sound of horse hooves filled the air. Without saying a word, Kit lifted the princess from the floor and threw her aboard Puzat making lifting a dead weight look effortless, even though it appeared the princess didn't seem to realise what was happening around her. Kit jumped on Puzat behind her. Daisy mounted Demon swiftly pulling the Mage up behind her.

"We need to get out of here quickly your men are dead," Daisy said with sorrow written on her face.

His brow furrowed, but before he could reply they had set off at a fast canter through the forest, weaving in and out of the line of trees, the branches making it difficult to see which way to go.

Murgo made a split-second decision to follow them; he climbed a tree and swept through the trees with grace. They could all hear the hoof beats behind them getting louder and louder, filling their ear drums with dread.

"We have to get out of the forest onto the track, it's too dense for this speed," Kit shouted over to Daisy who narrowly missed a yew tree.

Daisy nodded back in agreement as she struggled to regain control of the horse. The horses jumped on to the rutted track, the leaves fell to the ground like confetti around them. Kit turned to see the men dressed in red were in the forest, on the track behind them, right behind them, not giving in, never getting slower, just always there behind them.

"We need a clearing so we can see them; there won't be anywhere for them to hide then," Kit shouted to Daisy.

"Hopefully there will be one soon as the horses are tiring," Daisy replied, her voice getting lost in the sound of the hooves behind them.

They rounded a corner quickly to see a grassy area to the right leading to a small sloping hill. The Mage let out a sigh of relief as she had almost slipped off the back of Demon around the corner; she wasn't sure how long she would be able to hold on for. Kit signalled Daisy to head towards the grassland and to take the left where she would take the right, they churned the grass up, huge clumps of earth flew from the horse's hooves as they galloped up the hill.

Riding up the hill Kit whispered to Puzat to get the princess over the hill and to find safety; she gracefully somersaulted off the back of the galloping horse, landing neatly on her feet. The claws fully extended, ready for the onslaught of battle, however, the red demons had stopped at the bottom of the hill armed with arrows full of burning flames.

Murgo had stayed in the trees not knowing whether to

help or stay out of the way, when he saw Puzat and the Demon set off with the Mage and the princess he knew his job was to keep them safe.

"They really don't want her alive, do they? I'm getting bored of this now," Daisy said appearing next to Kit.

Kit smirked. "They are persistent; I want to know how much she is paying them."

"I imagine it is more then we will ever see, I might ask her for a job." Daisy laughed as the first set of arrows descended on them.

Kit dropped to the floor, spinning round in a circle with her claws embedded into the ground making a perfect circle. As she stood, she started chanting an ancient protection spell, the ground shook, the wind picked up and then silence as the arrows rained down on them.

Chapter Seventeen

Destin walked behind his brothers, listening to them chat excitedly about how they would take the kingdom, when suddenly the ground shook with such force he almost fell over, he grabbed the shirt of his brother to steady himself.

When the ground settled, silence followed. Destin looked around the confused faces of the men. Bjoarn spoke up, "We have to investigate the meaning of this, it appears to have begun over the hill." He pointed in that direction.

"Wait. Is that two horses running down the hill?" Destin asked, narrowing his eyes.

Bjoarn craned his neck to look into the distance to see that indeed there were two horses running at full speed down the hill.

"Who is in favour of seeing what the commotion is about?" Bjoarn asked the men who stared back at him with nodding heads.

The men put their hands up one after another looking around to see if anyone had objected which of course no one had, everyone seemed quite intrigued in what was happening over the hill which didn't surprise Destin as there hadn't been that much action compared to other voyages they had been on. They set off at a fast march across the grassland making sure not to step in any of the marshland that lurked beneath the long grass. As they reached the bottom of the hill, the two galloping horses nearly collided with them. Destin stared up at the rearing beast, he could swear he recognised the girl on the black horse who was trying to cling on to the wild-looking animal.

"Excuse us, please let us pass," the girl stammered slightly as she tried to sound in charge of the situation.

Bjoarn smiled at the girl but it wasn't a sincere smile where it reached his eyes, where they crinkle with joy, it was more of a sneer with a glint in his eye which made the girl pull her horse to the side and shout to the other girl, "Nekite, follow me." With a sharp kick the horses started galloping back up the hill to where they had come from.

The look in that rough-looking man's face made the Mage's heart hammer in her chest, her eyes streamed as the wind hit her face with such force she couldn't tell if she was crying or not, her brain was scrambled with panic. The feeling of dread that filled her entire being was threatening to overwhelm her. As the horses swiftly galloped back up the hill, she forced herself to look behind her, her eyes widened and she let out an involuntary squeal as she saw the men run full pelt behind them all shouting in a weird foreign language she couldn't understand. She looked over at the princess who sat clutched to Puzat's mane. She looked totally blank as if she wasn't aware what was happening to them. She urged Demon on faster but as she did so the horse tripped and the Mage became unseated, ending up in a bundle on the floor. Her heart hammered faster, so fast in fact, she was certain you could see it through her clothes; she struggled to get her breath back as the fall had completely winded her. As she tried to stand, she was knocked off of her feet with a blow to her side. She screamed out in pain as her whole side burned. Her eyes watered, she blinked back tears rapidly, she didn't want to appear weak in front of these men. She sat hunched down on the grass, not even daring to look up as she stared at the grass which was starting to sway in the breeze. Her mind rushed to all the possibilities of what was going to happen to her.

"Why the hell did you do that," Destin shouted at Bjoarn who had struck the girl across the ribs with the handle of his axe.

"She was going to escape," Bjoarn shouted back with a carefree shrug of the shoulder.

Destin shook his head in complete shock, he hadn't seen his brother lose his temper in that way in a while. It had seemed he had finally grown up but obviously not. When they were all younger Bjoarn was always getting into trouble for one thing or another whereas Destin was the more sensible one and Ethan was the quiet one who liked to stay in the background. Even though they looked similar, their personalities couldn't be more different.

"Enough!" the king boomed. He had been watching to see if his sons could sort out the problem that had arisen; it appeared that not one of them could sort it out. The king took a deep breath, exhaling loudly, sometimes he thought Bjoarn would make a great leader. However, at other times, he thought he was too hot-headed and reckless.

Ethan knelt down towards the girl and offered her his hand. "I am truly sorry about that my lady." He smiled at her, his long blonde hair gently moving in the breeze.

The Mage stood with his aid, looking into his dark green eyes. The Mage tried to figure out if it was okay to trust this man as a sharp pain shot through her side, making her clutch at her ribs and double over in pain.

"My friends are up there. I think they are in trouble," she whispered through gritted teeth as a tear slid down her face and the world went black.

Ethan simply scooped her up and started marching up the hill. Bjoarn and Destin both looked at him in awe as this was totally out of character. Ethan hated conflict between the brothers and usually left them to it.

The two brothers raised their eyebrows and shrugged their shoulders; they turned and looked towards the king who nodded in Ethan's direction indicating they should all follow. All the men reached the top of the hill and the scene that greeted them shocked them to the core. Some of the men screamed and ran, others fainted and some simply cried.

Chapter Eighteen

"Kit look at the hill," Daisy shouted over from where she was cutting another red devil's throat from ear to ear.

Kit looked towards the hill top and saw what seemed like another army of men, her heart sank slightly. "Jeez does it ever end," she shouted back.

Kit plunged her claws into the chest of another red devil. He slid to the ground in a heap with a slight moan of defeat. She stole a glance towards the hill top, she could definitely make out the shape of Puzat charging towards them. She raised her eyes to the sky and let out a groan of frustration.

The red devil leader looked on in astonishment at the carnage around him, these girls were good, and much to his displeasure they had to engage in hand-to-hand combat as the arrows they had been so confident in had simply failed to make contact with the woman who he assumed must be witches. He had rallied another twenty men which should have given them more of a chance of destroying these girls and dispatching the princess. He dreaded to think what Eva would do if they didn't succeed.

"We have to pull back and sort that out," Daisy shouted, jumping over a dead red devil and pointing to the hilltop.

"Agreed, I'll catch Puzat," Kit replied, running up the hill.

She grabbed hold of the reins and soothed the panting horse, the sweat rolling off him in huge droplets. The princess slipped off him immediately, Kit just managing to catch her before she fell to the floor.

"Daisy, hurry up, we need to get up the hill!" Kit shouted over to Daisy who had jumped on the back of an unfortunate red devil and was biting through his neck, the blood soaking her through.

Kit threw the princess over her shoulder and started to run as fast as she could up the hill, with the added weight of the princess her progress was slow, allowing Daisy to catch up quickly.

"Look over there." Daisy stopped and pointed towards the wooded area just after the grassland.

Kit's eyes scanned the woodland catching sight of red clothing flashing through the trees.

"There's more?" she asked in an exclaimed voice shuffling the princess further on her shoulder.

"We can't fight them and those men on top of the hill, I mean, we're good but not that good, and unfortunately I am pretty certain they have the Mage," Daisy said, squinting her eyes to try get a better look at the bundle in one of the strange looking men's arms.

Kit mused for a second, which felt like an eternity to Daisy, before replying slowly, "We need help. I could ask them to help." She nodded with a creased brow at Daisy who smiled and started to take the princess from Kit's shoulders.

A few moments later Kit had dragged a red devil up to where Daisy was stood. He was beginning to take his last breaths but he would have to do for their sacrifice, Kit cut through his neck spilling more blood onto the floor. She dropped the body on the floor and started to recite the words to the god Osiris. Kit started to chant quietly with Daisy joining in until they were shouting in frenzy. The red devils seemed to be reforming with the men who had just entered from the woodland.

"I don't want to rush you but they're getting ready to attack," Daisy said, breaking the chant for a split second then carrying on. Ideally Kit needed more people to chant, but with the princess in her catatonic state, she and Daisy would have to do it alone.

Kit had only done this a handful of times, the first time she had successfully achieved raising an army of the dead had been on one particular bloody battle in the south of the kingdom, and it had looked like the king's army were to be defeated for the first time in history.

Daisy could remember running as fast as she could, body slamming Kit, knocking her off her feet just in time as a spear flew through the air narrowly missing them. Daisy lay there with heavy breathing trying to catch her breath whilst Kit was trying to push her off.

"I think you winded me." Kit struggled to speak, clutching her chest. "Huh, saved your life though," Daisy snarkily replied, coughing a little.

Kit managed to smile back. Even in the circumstances they were a great team, she was about to speak when another set of arrows started to fall from the sky. Both Kit and Daisy shielded themselves with a dead soldier, huddling together in the blood-soaked ground. The arrows eventually stopped, and as the two girls looked up, they saw the king upon his white horse with mud and blood splattered all over it surrounded by the enemy. They were circling him, shouting and jabbing their swords towards the horse which kept shying and rearing away.

Daisy stood up and looked around her at the carnage that lay at their feet. She realised they were the only ones left, everyone else had been killed. She took a deep sigh, the arrows had killed off anyone who had tried to run. Panic threatened to take over her. It rose in her stomach making her feel quite nauseous. She gulped in air, tears prickled her eyes, she was certain they would die today. But as she stood there watching the king getting taunted by the enemy Kit started to chant.

Daisy was unable to move, her head was telling her to go help Kit but her body was not moving. She stared unblinking at the hundreds of dead men clawing, climbing and dragging themselves out of the cracks that tore through the earth. Tears started to run down her cheeks as her heart rate escalated to a new high as the men stared back at her with empty eye sockets just a black hole reaching into their skull. Some of their jaws hung loose from their skulls giving them a jaunty lopsided toothy grin, some had tufts of rotting hair attached to their heads where others were completely skeletal. She tried to scream but no sound came out as she stood there shaking involuntarily trying to get a grip with what she was seeing, suddenly Kit looked around and smiled stopping the chanting to shout, "Attack!"

The enemy had stopped taunting the king and simply stopped deathly still watching the dead men run towards them with rusty mud-clad weapons. Most of the enemy turned and ran in the opposite direction, a few of these men fainted with fear and only a few of the braver ones took a defensive stance ready for the onslaught of battle.

Daisy watched in shock, fear and something she thought might be admiration for Kit as she quietly led the king's sweat-drenched horse with the king slumped upon it awkwardly away from the horde of the living and dead warriors.

Daisy shook her head a little to get rid of the memory that plagued her thoughts as the ground shook, huge cracks ravaged the landscape, and the rotted skeletal hands clawed their way to the surface once more for a different battle this time.

Destin couldn't move his legs which were rigid to the spot, he didn't think he had felt fear like this before, however, his eyes couldn't be torn away from the scene being played out in front of them. His eyes were naturally drawn to the white-haired girl with metal-like claws coming straight out of her hands. He was mesmerized by her. His heart beat galloped within his chest. He felt a weird sensation when he looked at the girl, a sensation he couldn't put a name to. He couldn't hear his brothers telling him to run or even feel them pushing and shoving around him he was that mesmerized by the scene.

"Destin, we have to move now!" Bjoarn shouted, grabbing Destin's arms and shaking them hard, terror in his eyes which he wasn't trying to hide.

Destin blinked several times, coming out of his trance in time to watch Ethan begin to turn round, heading back down the hill with the girl nestled protectively in his arms when, seemingly out of nowhere, a purple-haired girl with pure purple eyes leapt on his back. He watched Ethan crumple to the ground, it seemed to Destin everything was happening in slow motion and he couldn't quite compute what was happening, however, before the girl wielding the axe in the air could strike his brother, he grabbed her wrist. He blinked hard several times staring into the swirl of purple that stared back at him.

"That is enough," he said with a strong voice which didn't portray how scared he actually was.

The girls pupilless eyes bore into his own, he wondered if those eyes could see through to his soul. She stared at him for what felt like hours. He could barely breathe as he watched metal fangs slide out of her mouth and past her chin. Just as he thought she was surely going to kill them all he heard a cough.

"So you have something that doesn't belong to you." The white-haired girl who had been bringing the dead alive, smiled, pointing towards the girl wrapped in a bundle underneath Ethan.

Destin stuttered, "We didn't harm her!" in a slightly higher than normal voice.

The white-haired girl cocked her head slightly and smiled in a soothing sort of way which Destin wanted to trust.

"Hello Daisy and Kit, I think I fainted," came a muffled voice.

"Are you okay?" Daisy replied to the Mage, still snarling at the Vikings.

"My ribs hurt a little but other than that no harm came to me," she replied, peering round the huge shoulder that protected her.

Kit looked down the hill for a split second. "We shall speak about this later, but now I think we should move and move fast." She flashed everyone another warming smile. "Can you walk?" she directed the question at the Mage.

"She can, but she can't run, I will take care of her." Ethan stood up, still grasping hold of the Mage.

Kit looked over at Daisy seeking answers as to what to do next, however, the only response given was the dangerous glint from her fangs. Kit let her shoulders drop slightly, this situation was becoming increasingly difficult. She rubbed her temple slightly.

"I don't suppose one of you could carry the other girl for us as the horses need a rest," she spoke to them, her voice becoming warmer and warmer in an effort to relax everyone. Destin heard himself say, "Of course I will carry her," following her and lifting the dead weight of the seemingly simple girl.

"Thank you, right, I suggest we make a swift exit," Kit replied.

They all headed down the hill as fast they could without stumbling, tripping or hurting themselves. Kit kept glancing behind her making sure they weren't being followed. She could hear the clash of swords, the shouts and roars from falling men, it was this sound that pushed her on faster. Once at the bottom of the hill she took in great gulps of air trying to get her breath back, resisting the urge to bend over and rest her hands on her knees. Daisy nudged her, she turned her head to the right to see more men who wore their beards long and plaited. Kit's eyes widened for a second.

"I seriously hope they are with you," Kit asked Destin who was still holding the princess.

All the man could do was nod, Kit raised her eyebrow and let out a little sigh. She just wanted this all to be over, but in her heart, she knew they had a long way to go.

"Good, right let's keep moving, any idea which way though?" Daisy said, placing a hand over her eyes as if she was scanning the terrain.

"We should be safe in the mountains," the Mage replied, still in the arms of that man. Daisy glanced at the Mage checking if she was safe.

"Unfortunately, we will be unable to accompany you," the huge Bjoarn, with bigger muscles than all of the other men, grunted out, his red hair looking like flames protruding from his head.

"But," Destin tried to interrupt whilst rearranging the princess in his arms.

"We are on a course for the palace so we shall have to leave you here," the massive Bjoarn just carried on talking over him.

"Oh, and who are you?" Daisy asked, raising an eyebrow and crossing her arms defensively. "I am Bjoarn son of King Ake," the man said pointedly.

Before Daisy could retaliate, Kit cut in, "It's not safe for anyone to be going to the palace at the moment with those red warriors about, unfortunately they have spotted you with us, that now makes you the enemy to them, as you have seen for yourselves, they are not very pleasant. We need to get as much ground cover between them and us." She smiled then quickly looked over her shoulder towards the top of the hill.

There was a pause for a second as all of them saw the red warriors line up at the top of the hill, pointing their swords in the air.

"Agreed," said both men in unison, holding the princess and the Mage tightly to them.

Before Bjoarn could reply, Kit and Daisy marched past him, grabbed the reins of the horses and started to march off towards the rocky terrain of the mountain region, glancing back to see that the warriors were simply staring them out from the top of the hill, sending a shiver down both of the girls' backs.

Chapter Nineteen

The procession of people walked easily together, chatting happily, once the threat of the red warriors had passed. Destin caught up with the white-haired girl. He couldn't help but stare at her, never taking his eyes from her.

"I was just wondering if I may know your name?" he stuttered slightly at the sight of her electric blue eyes that contained no pupils.

She smiled at him. "The name is Kit, that is Daisy." Pointing at her. "That is the Mage." Who was still snuggled in Ethan's arms. "And that is Nekite." Pointing to the princess who was now in Bjoarn's arms.

"I'm Destin, I am also the son of King Ake." He smiled at her. "I guess you wonder why we are here," he asked with a rub of his temple.

"It had crossed my mind that you weren't from around here." She laughed lightly, looking up at him, which made his heart skip a few beats.

"Our father's aim is to overthrow the king and claim the land as his, me and my brothers would take over the throne," he blurted out.

Kit stopped walking and looked at him intently, cocking her head to the side slightly. "Many have tried that and failed. I have it seen it many times. They are scared of this kingdom." She carried on walking, her thoughts whizzing around her head going a million miles per hour.

"I have heard of god-like creatures that roam the land. They are said to protect the king but we are strong and my brother never loses a fight," he replied walking side by side.

"Well for now your father will have to put his plans on hold until we sort this mess out." He nodded in the direction of the princess wrapped in Bjoarn's arms.

Destin carried on walking in silence next to Kit; he played with different thoughts as to why these girls were being hunted by the red warriors, occasionally glancing towards Kit, trying to read her expression.

Murgo had watched on from the safety of the trees, his brain not wanting to believe what his eyes had seen. His hand had been resting on his sword twitching nervously at the sight. Maybe his men had been right about the girls? Maybe they were bad omens for his clan? However, he still couldn't shake the feeling that they needed him, that his fate was entwined with theirs. As he crouched on the tree branch watching the girls leading the group of men, he knew he had to follow from a distance keeping his watchful eye over them.

"Where did Murgo go in all that kerfuffle?" Daisy asked, craning her neck around to see if she spotted him anywhere.

"My guess would be back to the forest to his people, he stuck to his word. He did lead us out of the forest," Kit replied, keeping her eye on the princess.

Daisy nodded a reply, keeping her head down as they trudged through the meadow. Kit looked at Daisy. "I'm sure we will meet him again." She smiled as she said it.

Daisy nodded back. "I am feeling pretty tired, this on the run thing we seem to be doing is exhausting." She let out a long sigh.

"I agree we just need to keep it going until the princess is safely back, I am also concerned about these men and who they are," Kit quietened her voice as she spoke.

Daisy replied without raising her head, "Yes, I have the same concerns, I would like to know how the Mage has been injured, it looks like broken ribs to me." Daisy sighed again. "Nightfall will be interesting."

They had walked for what seemed like miles. The group had travelled across quaint little streams, never-ending rows of meadows and passing by eerie-looking woodland. Up and down hills, over hard, cracked, ground and soggy marshland. Through rain and then startling sunlight. Eventually, when Kit thought that Daisy wouldn't be able to walk another step, they came across a cave that the Mage seemed very excited about.

At first, they had almost walked straight past the entrance as a huge boulder hid the cave from any unsuspecting people. To the left of the boulder there was a small crevice. Water trickled down the side of the crevice, making the rocky side slippery. Kit peered through the gap in the rock and the slippery steps which had been carved into the stone.

"I hope the horses can get through this gap," she said, peering at the gap closely.

"Yes, don't worry we can roll the boulder slightly to fit them through, we do it with the revolt's ponies," the Mage replied, being set down by Ethan.

The Mage clutched her side as she slithered through the gap, the darkness enveloped her immediately, and Kit studied Ethan's face. She watched as worry crept across his facial features. It occurred to Kit that the man had grown fond of the Mage whilst he had carried her all these miles, they had chatted to one another nonstop which she thought was very sweet. Even though it made her smile, it did create a pang of jealousy that flared up momentarily in her chest. She would love if someone could look and feel something like that for her, but as she studied her hands, she ran her fingers over her knuckles where the claws protruded out of the rough skin creating texture that surely no one could love.

"Kit, are you coming," Daisy said, nudging her shoulder.

Kit looked up in surprise as Daisy stood in front of her frowning.

"You were in your own world then." She laughed slightly, pointing her finger at her.

"Sorry." Kit shook her head. "I will follow the Mage if you lead the horses." She smiled at Daisy in an effort to reassure her. Daisy nodded back, grabbing the reins of the horses.

The passageway was narrow, dark and damp. The smell of stagnant water hit Kit like a wall, it was almost repulsive making her retch slightly. She could touch both sides of the passageway. As she carried on up the inclining slippery steps, she climbed up and up spotting spiders and small furies crawling around making her stifle a cry. She almost lost her footing on the crumbling step as she sidestepped around a small dark creature. Kit started to think the dark passageway was never ending until a shaft of light broke through, making the water running down the sides of the rocky cliffs almost sparkle.

"I can see light," she said almost breathlessly.

"Good I was beginning to panic we were stuck in here, have you seen the size of the spiders in here?" Daisy replied in between heavy breaths.

"I'm trying not to look if I'm honest," she replied with a

shudder.

Kit reached the opening of the passageway and gulped down fresh air as Daisy joined her. "Remind me never to do that again," Daisy said with an involuntary shudder.

Kit was about to agree when the Mage, who had climbed onto a tall rock to get a vague sense of direction, jumped down and winced in pain. She clutched her side and took deep breaths.

"So are you going to tell me what happened?" Daisy said after finally getting her breath back. The Mage looked at the floor absentmindedly moving a twig around the dirt with her foot. "Well…" Daisy said again this time with more force.

The Mage sighed. "We were going down the hill when we came across the men." She paused for a brief second. "I admit I was scared, so I decided we should come back up the hill but they began to chase us. I fell from Demon when she stumbled and as I got up, one of the men struck me which has hurt my ribs," she spluttered the words out as fast as she could, not daring to look up to see if Daisy was judging her.

Instead, she felt arms around her as she was drawn into a hug.

"Do you think you remember which one of the men hit you?" Daisy said into the Mage's hair.

The Mage nodded. "The one carrying the princess."

Daisy detached herself from the Mage and looked directly into the eyes of the man that had injured the Mage. Instinctively her fangs shot out, her purple eyes appearing to shine more brightly. Daisy could see the realisation cross his face as she snarled at him. She stepped around the Mage and walked purposely over to him. She caught Kit's confused expression out of the corner of her eye, she would have to explain later.

"I think we need to have a chat," she barked at Bjoarn.

He clutched the catatonic princess to his chest as if she would protect him from the wrath of Daisy.

"I can't imagine why," he managed to say without stuttering.

She smiled sweetly at him then, suddenly with no warning, twisted him sideways and jabbed him in the side with such force the sound of bones crunching could be heard, then twisted him back to face forwards. She did all that so quickly Bjoarn didn't have time to react. He stood stock still in so much shock that the only reaction was the blink of his eyes.

"I hope next time you will think about the consequences of your actions," Daisy said, turning away from him flicking her hair.

Daisy walked past Kit and as she did so she turned her head slightly. "Nice to see you making friends," Kit said under her breath.

Daisy merely shrugged her shoulders and once again joined the Mage at the other side of the pathway. "Just need to put them in their place sometimes." She sighed. "So which way now?"

The Mage glanced around her surroundings, making sure not to give Bjoarn eye contact, her cheeks flushed pink from witnessing Daisy striking him; she smiled slightly at the thought. She pulled herself together giving herself a mental shake. She raised her hand in the air whilst calling for the bird, for a moment there was silence just the breeze swirling around them. After a second or two the elegant creature swooped down from above, gliding elegantly through the air and dropping effortlessly on to the Mage's outreached arm. She whispered to the bird with a smile on her face. As the bird took off again, the huge wingspan nearly knocking the mage to the rocky ground, the mage steadied herself clutching her burning ribs. She whispered the ancient ritualistic words Cumemec Hræfnwann, the moment the words left her mouth her eyes turned as black as the night sky. The Viking men stepped back in alarm at the sight of a small girl controlling a huge bird, the Mage was unaware of the men's faces as all she could see was the leafy tree tops amid the rocky terrain as the bird glided through the air.

The bird dived into the wooded area, swooping around the trunks of the trees, suddenly flying through a narrow crevice between two rocks. The Mage had the bird fly close to the floor, searching for any tracks which the remaining revolt members might have left behind. She was about to give up when the bird flew past something that caught her attention. The mage furrowed her brow whilst she directed the bird around again. The bird hovered in the air, claws outstretched above a scrap of material, she smiled and the bird swooped down and clutched the material between the impressive talons.

"I am pretty sure I have found the way, we need to go through the trees, through a gap between two boulders and then along a small track," she said to the group, nodding her head.

She turned her attention again on the bird as it soared through the air, whizzing past rocky terrain, boulders and trees. The Mage was secretly hoping she would get a glimpse of the revolt, but as the bird flew faster, and further into the mountains, she couldn't spot them. She let out a frustrated sigh, her fist clenched as the thought they might have lied to her entered her head. She was about to return the bird when she saw a wooden bucket next to what looked like the end of a stream, her heart beat quickened as the bird flew low along the trickling stream, its reflection shining and glistening in the sunlight. And that's when the Mage saw them. Her whole face lit up.

The Mage saw the people she regarded as family, they were milling around doing their daily tasks, simply getting on with their days. The Mage's whole face lit up at the simplicity of their lives compared to what she had just lived through. She perched the bird on a low-hanging branch for a few seconds so she could gather her thoughts and relish in the fact these people so dear to her weren't dead. They were alive and the note which she had secretly feared was false hadn't been a lie or a trap at all.

Destin walked over to Kit. "How is the Mage doing?" He stared at her with concern.

"I haven't actually seen this before so it's all new for me," Kit replied with a quiet giggle, she distractedly rubbed her head.

Destin was silent for a few seconds mulling over a few thoughts when he blurted out, "So I have been thinking of that battle you had with those red men?"

Kit tilted her head towards him, the low evening sun blinding her vision. "I did wonder when you would ask some questions. I am surprised it's taken this long."

He gave a short laugh. "Did I really watch you raise the army of the dead?" He managed to look directly at her but got no answer from her blue pools of eyes.

She smiled, closed her eyes for a brief second, and replied, "Yes you did see me do that, you are aware of the gods who protect this kingdom, you have said as much already." She looked questioningly at him.

He merely nodded a response.

"I am one of those so-called gods and so is Daisy," she said, tilting her head in Daisy's direction, "but in actual fact we are just regular people," she concluded.

A soft snort escaped his mouth. "I don't mean to offend you but where I come from regular people don't look like you." He frowned slightly, worried he had overstepped the line and would be treated in the same manner as Bjoarn who was still nursing his side.

Kit simply laughed. "I am sure you are quite right, it's such a long story it will bore you."

As Kit stood there watching the Mage zone out, her own thoughts drifted off into a place she didn't let them go frequently. She had thought, even hoped, she had locked these memories away. But as they trickled out, they filled her vision with horrors only Daisy would understand.

Chapter Twenty

Kit looked down at her hands, the pain was mind numbing. It was like a fire burning her every nerve: stars danced and surrounded her eyesight. She felt she couldn't see straight. She clutched her head between her hands. She stumbled to the ground several times, landing on soft white padding, her eyes trickled as her head hung low as if too heavy for her body. Droplets of blood ran down her face and hit the floor leaving a bright red spot which was such a contrast to the stark white around her. She fell to the ground again, landing on her hands, the shooting fire-like pain flew up her arms. She screamed out in pain. As despair threatened to overwhelm her, four metal-like claws protruded through her hand. A queasy feeling erupted in her stomach as she sat staring at the metal-like claws.

She vaguely heard something or someone trying to get her attention.

"Kit we need to carry on, the Mage has found where the revolt members are." Destin looked at her with even more concern etched across his face.

"Are you okay? You seemed miles away?" he asked gently, searching her face for any clues.

She forced a smile. "Of course I am okay, I am a god after all," she said with a laugh, and he laughed back.

The Mage led the way almost gleefully skipping in front

before she abruptly stopped and regarded Ethan with an intense stare. It knocked him off guard.

"I have been thinking." She paused for a brief second. "I wondered if you would help us?" She turned slightly towards him.

"Help in what way, and who may us be?" He arched one eyebrow in response.

"You would be helping my family, the revolt, you see I came across the gods when we tried to ambush them. The revolt needed them to help overthrow the king you see." She was nodding as if it all made perfect sense.

Ethan simply stared at her, his footing momentarily lost. "You mean the gods are real?" His eyebrow creased with doubt as he righted himself. "I have so many questions," he finished.

She nodded at him. "Yes, of course they are real. Who do you think Kit and Daisy are?" She stopped walking and clutched her side, getting her breath back. She didn't want to admit it was difficult to breathe.

"Surely you can't think they are normal?" She carried on walking, trying to hide her laboured breathing.

He sighed, glancing at the two girls who were chatting and leading their horses, clearly joking around with one another.

"Well, their appearance is different, but this kingdom is so very strange who is to say what is considered normal." He smiled at her and before she could respond, said, "And do not think I haven't seen you struggling with your side.," With that he swooped her up in his arms effortlessly and marched ahead.

"I can manage. I do not need help," she told him haughtily, but she didn't resist the strong arms around her.

"Well, we will get there quicker this way," he responded easily. "And on another note, if they are gods, why would you want to ambush them?"

The Mage sighed at him as if he was a small child not understanding her. "Because they are the only ones strong enough to help us overthrow the king. That is where I was hoping you would help, the more manpower we have the better chance we have of succeeding," she concluded, her voice laced with pride for their plans.

Ethan kept looking ahead as he spoke, "We shall see, my father has plans of his own."

The Mage glanced up, trying to read his expression, taking in everything about him from his fair hair to his long beard encased in leather twine, to his tattoo on his left side of his scalp. She hoped this man who had carried her away from danger would help them secure the future of their kingdom.

Eva heard another knock on her door. She sighed with annoyance. This better be the red devil general with good news. She had struggled getting into the princess's dress as she could have used an extra pair of hands to do the corset up, but she guessed it looked authentically dishevelled being only half done up.

She crossed the small, dimly-lit room quickly. "Who is there?" she called out quietly, knowing full well who would answer.

"Madam it is I, the general," he stated in a resigned tone that grated through Eva. She could already sense she wasn't going to be best pleased with the news.

She turned the rusty key and shoved the heavy oak door open. She peered down the dark corridors, seeing they were alone, she ushered the general in.

"Please, sit down, you look exhausted," she said. directing him to the barrel across the room.

"I am here to report that we haven't managed to dispatch them again." He stared at the floor, not daring to look up.

Eva's face darkened to almost thunder. She took a deep breath in an effort to control her anger. Her eye twitched involuntary at the effort of it.

He started to stutter out an excuse when she abruptly raised her hand to silence him.

"I really hope for you and your men this is good," she snapped through gritted teeth.

She sat down, arranging her shredded dress attentively, waiting to hear the news. She drummed her fingers against her knees in anticipation.

"I won't beat around the bush, they raised the army of the dead. We stood no chance, they just kept coming." He quickly glanced up then looked at the floor.

Eva let out a deep breath which whistled through her teeth.

"I just want them dead…" She clenched and unclenched her hands in quick succession, not sure whether to strike the man in front of her or not.

"Perhaps we have scared them off enough not to return?" the man ventured quietly.

"That may be the case, but nothing is to stop them eventually coming back and ruining my plans," she seethed.

She stood up and started to pace the room, muttering to herself. After a while she stopped, turned to the red devil general, and stated, "Fine we are running out of time for this plan to succeed, therefore I will go on as intended, I will appoint you my personal security, it will be your job to find them and kill them." She looked up into the weary eyes of the man who merely nodded a response.

The princess still hadn't stirred when they had arrived at the abandoned bucket collecting fresh water from the stream. Daisy looked at the princess, cradled by the brute of the man who she had struck, she mused. He seemed to be taking good care of the princess. It did occur to her this could be due to the fact he might have figured out who the princess was.

She giggled to herself or he might be scared of her.

"Where now?" she called out to the Mage diverting her attention. "Just follow me, I can hear them chatting away." She smiled at Daisy.

The Mage jumped down from Ethan and scrambled across fallen rocks. She slid into the clear trickling stream. The water flowed over her boots, soaking her socks through. The water felt refreshing, even cleansing. She stopped a second to let the cooling water flow around her and sooth her.

Ethan shouted for her to be careful as she waded through the water, but she was concentrating on the noise up ahead, children laughing with the odd playful shriek filled the air. Daisy jumped in the water after her, her fangs instinctively shot out, her senses heightened, she glanced back at Kit who also had her claws out. The men soon followed with the horses bringing up the rear, all stumbling on the river bed rocks. Daisy cried out at the Mage who had fallen to her knees, soaking her dress through, but she didn't care. She climbed up the bank and ran towards the revolt members, they had stopped going about their daily tasks, stood stock still in surprise and fear at the amount of people coming out of the river. The Mage stood facing them, the smile slipping from her face. Her eyebrows creased together, confusion replacing the smile. She looked from Daisy to Kit, who had joined her at her side. Suddenly the silence broke, a woman screamed in the distance, then mass panic erupted. Men picked up anything they could find, tools, stones, even cooking utensils ready to fight.

"No, no, it is I, the Mage," she shouted, shaking her head, her hands up in surrender. The revolt member's men surged forward bellowing as they did so.

"Why is everyone so violent at the moment," Daisy muttered to herself, exasperated.

The Mage backed away and bumped into Ethan who reached for his sword, then a loud booming voice stopped everyone in their tracks.

"Enough fighting. There has been too much bloodshed as it is," a tall cloaked man boomed.

No one dared to speak for a few seconds until the Mage cleared her throat, stepping away from the protection of Ethan. "It is I, the Mage." She paused for a brief moment clearing her throat. "I have completed the task required of me. I found the gods. They have travelled with me on this long journey." She faltered slightly, looking at Kit and then Daisy.

Daisy lifted her lips up slightly in an effort to smile whereas Kit simply nodded her head. "These men are going to help us." She looked back towards the group behind her.

The tall cloaked man's eyes stared into Daisy's and Kit's huge pools of swirling emptiness that were their eyes. He was trying to intimidate them, trying to reach into their minds, trying to read their intentions.

Daisy let out a snort of laughter smirking at him.

Kit simply smiled at him. "I would be careful trying that, you will get lost in there."

He frowned then blinked back at her, eventually diverting his attention back to the Mage, who had begun to shiver under her soaking clothes.

He plastered a fake smile across his weather-beaten face.

"Well done, you must need to rest, then we shall talk about what is to be done." With that he turned and walked away.

"He seems friendly," Daisy said, as her fangs retracted into her head.

"The whole place seems friendly," Kit replied, with a lopsided sarcastic grin.

Kit rubbed her eyes, wearily looking towards Destin, who shrugged his shoulders in confusion; this wasn't quite the welcome any of them had expected.

The Mage had turned towards them, distractedly playing with her sodden dress and looking at the floor, she spoke so softly both Kit and Daisy had to lean in to hear.

"I assume the welcome committee we had here, is the result of the loss we have suffered, I hope tomorrow will be better for us." She kept her eyes on the floor, nodding to herself.

With that, a scruffy peasant-looking girl appeared from nowhere, directing them to little wooden huts set into the mountain side; the wood of which the huts were made was starting to rot in places and the thatched roof sagged with the pressure of fallen rocks. Tree roots littered the path almost making a staircase, earthenware pots lay scattered around the outside of the huts as if misplaced. To the right of the hut there was an even more dishevelled looking farm building which the horses were to be kept in. Daisy arched an eyebrow at the sight of the wonky door and the offensive odour. However, Kit took in the sight, smiling to herself. This little part of the kingdom almost felt like heaven to her. She had dreamed of this sort of life for so long, to be free, to do what she wanted when she wanted. She let out a little sigh.

The revolt member showed them through the door. She let them know that the stream was the only water source and food was stored in barrels near the leader's hut. The food was rationed as well. Which didn't go down well with the Viking men as their appetite was vast. The girl bowed her head slightly to Kit and Daisy and scurried off. Kit glanced around the dark damp little room which she was to share with the others. Her smiled broadened at the state of the place they were to call home.

Bjoarn placed the princess on the straw mattress in the corner. "I think we need to sort this girl out, what happened to her?" he directed the question to Kit not daring to look at Daisy.

Kit stared at the princess for a second before answering, "She is Princess Nekite, daughter of the king of this kingdom. Unfortunately, she has seen things that someone in her position should not see." Kit paused for a second. "Those red warriors were sent to kill her, I am, however, hopeful she will be okay as the kingdom is in great danger without her."

Bjoarn stared down at the princess with surprise. "I didn't realize who she was," he said with utter disbelief.

Kit replied kindly, "Well her clothes are very lavish, that should have given it away."

He nodded a response. "What happened to you all?" he asked, with a questioning tone, taking in the sight of the blue eyes and the white hair.

"That's a story for after we have rested," Kit replied, turning to get the princess a drink of water.

She stepped outside, having to shield her eyes from the bright sunlight; it was such a comparison from the dark little hut. She breathed in the clean fresh air and the sunlight made her hair almost translucent.

"The old man requested a meeting with all of us after supper." Destin came up behind her speaking softly.

Kit jumped in surprise, her mind had completely wandered off so she hadn't noticed Destin walking up to her.

"I was hoping it would it be tomorrow so we were well rested but never mind." Kit sighed heavily.

"I get the feeling we are not welcome." Destin looked around at the revolt members cautiously.

"Which is strange seeing as they need us," remarked Kit with another sigh.

Destin looked at her, the sun shining upon her eyes making them dazzling bright, he smiled shyly to himself. He knew whatever was to happen he would follow her to the end of it.

After supper, which consisted of gruel and stale bread, Kit, Daisy, the Mage, Destin, Ethan, Bjoarn and the princess all made their way to the leader's hut which was set aside from the other huts under a cluster of small trees. They all hesitated at the shabby rotten door which hung on its hinges at a jaunty angle. A fusty smell radiated from the hut which caught in the back of Daisy's throat. After a few seconds, Daisy glanced around the group, all of which were shifting their weight not wanting to be the one to knock.

"I'll knock then, shall I?" She rolled her eyes at them.

She stepped forward and knocked loudly. She paused for a second before opening the door, not waiting for a response.

The small group followed Daisy into the dark space, making the room even smaller. Kit was pressed between Daisy and Destin. She was very aware of Destin's body next to her, every time she shifted her weight, she accidentally brushed his arm or caught his hand near hers. She wanted to glance at him, to look into his eyes, but she stayed focused on the old man before them.

The old man spoke slowly but meaningfully.

"I am the revolt's leader, before this title I had a very different title: I was the king's brother. I refer to that in past tense due to the fact he tried to have me killed." He paused for dramatic effect.

Daisy rolled her eyes at him. "Oh, do go on, I do love a good story," she drawled at him. Kit nudged her sharply with her elbow without taking her eyes off the old man.

He carried on, ignoring Daisy's interruption, "My brother the king has led this kingdom into ruin. The people are poor, famine is high, it is a disgrace. Therefore, the king needs to be dispatched. That is where you two come into this story," he finished off staring at Daisy intently.

Daisy stared back at him, unmoved by his speech, she crossed her arms over her chest. "And what makes you think we will help you?"

"I am assuming the Mage has informed you that you are not free, you will never be free from the kingdom, you need this as much as I do." He coughed. "I mean we all need this." He glanced around the room looking for any acknowledgement.

Kit kept her face a mask, showing no emotion even though her mind was in turmoil, it was as if there was an internal battle going on within her. Every fibre of her being wanted to run away with Daisy into the wilderness never to be seen again, but she knew she couldn't leave these people like this. She knew she had to help them, as if every event in her life had led up to this.

The revolt leader looked upon them, surrounded by his dark cloak, his beady eyes poking out from the darkness. An uneasy feeling landed in the pit of Kit's stomach. She knew she could not trust this man, however much he preached about the good of the kingdom.

Daisy cleared her throat. "I am afraid you will have to give us time to consider what you are proposing."

"I was expecting nothing less," the leader said, turning away insinuating that the meeting was over.

They all filed out one after another into the dark night sky. The moon shone bright, illuminating the path back to their own little wooden shack. Bjoarn carried on holding the princess close to his chest. Even though she didn't bring anything to that meeting, in her catatonic state, it was thought best they didn't leave her as it was unclear who they could trust. Even though Daisy had expressed concerns to Kit regarding how much they could trust the Viking men. The group stood in the darkness for a few minutes all trying to process what they had heard tonight. As they did so, Kit watched Bjoarn with the princess. She seriously hoped he wasn't going to use the princess as a bargaining tool in whatever plans their king had. She rubbed her head distractedly, she must have a chat with the men.

Kit suddenly felt a hand on her arm. Daisy was tugging her into the shadows as the others wearily made their way to the hut.

"What are your thoughts?" Daisy asked, looking vaguely into the distance.

"Confusion." Kit laughed slightly. "To be honest I am

unsure what to do. I love the idea of just disappearing, but then the thought of making this kingdom great again overshadows it." She furrowed her brow.

"We won't be able to relax knowing we could have done something," Daisy pointed out, flicking her hair over her shoulder and pulling her cloak around her.

"I am concerned about the men's plan, it is obvious they were here for the kingdom." Kit's head slumped slightly as if the pressure had got too much.

"I agree, but I think we will come to face that challenge when it happens." She glanced at Kit before carrying on, "Anyway, I think that Destin likes you, so I am sure he wouldn't cross you." She smiled gleefully.

Kit's face coloured slightly but under the dark night sky it was not noticeable.

"He is not, he is simply intrigued about what we are." Kit shrugged her shoulder as if she couldn't care less but deep in her stomach butterflies started to flutter.

Chapter Twenty-One

That night the sky was clear, the moon shone bright, the wolves howled, the owls hooted: the forest was alive with anticipation as if it knew what was about to take place. Murgo crouched in a tree listening to all the sounds around him letting the noise embrace him; he had followed the girls as best he could whilst sticking to the safety of his beloved forest. He feared for all the girls' safety. He had not seen men such as these ones before with their long, plaited beards, and arms brandished with deep dark tattoos. However, the more Murgo had followed and watched he came to understand these men meant no further harm to the girls. It was indeed the red devils they had to watch for. He was still reeling from the sight of the battle. The one consolation was Murgo hadn't spotted one of those warriors since then but he had no doubt they would be back looking for more blood. He had waited several hours before he ventured up the crevice behind the boulder just in case there were watchmen.

Once inside the small dark damp space his nerves started to jitter slightly. The smell crept up his nose, making him retch. He steadied himself against the rough stone, a huge hairy spider ran across his hand. He snatched his hand back, instantly increasing his pace until he was running up the steps. He stumbled, tripped and fell through the opening at the top of the stairway, gulping back fresh air, his raised heart rate dropping steadily as he looked around his surroundings. He saw idyllic scenery consisting of rocks, trees and shrubs. He dropped to the floor, inspecting the dirt, letting it run through his fingers; he raised it so he could smell the gravel. He turned slightly, before spotting hoof prints, a smile spread across his tired face. He followed the hoof prints down a track through two boulders until he hit a stream. He turned to his left, then his right, but saw nothing. No tracks, no foot prints, no clues. His chest rose and fell in a sigh. He almost felt defeated. Maybe his men were right, maybe he should have just returned to his clan, weariness took over him his legs suddenly felt heavy, making him kneel on the stream's banks. As he sat staring into the trickling stream, he caught a glimpse of disturbed rock bed. He put his hand in the cool clear water, letting it run over his blue arm. He made his way into the water, trekking up the stream, stumbling slightly on the rock bed. He scrambled up the stream bank to find he was looking at a misshapen rotten hut. He cocked his head, a frown sweeping his forehead. At first, he thought they must be abandoned but as he got closer to the huts, he saw the signs of dying fires, cooking pots and when he listened carefully he could hear the shuffles of animals.

Murgo had inspected every hut in the small enclosure, looking for clues of the girls, until he spotted the horses resting lazily in the byre. He went up to them, letting them nuzzle him. He decided to rest with the horses. He arranged the straw into a small mound, resting his head. He was awoken by voices nearing the byre. From his view he could see the gods talking. As Kit walked towards the most dishevelled hut, Daisy stood alone looking into the distance. He gracefully hopped over the door. He tried to creep up on her, but there was no point, Daisy had swung round, fangs out ready for attack.

"It is only I." Murgo held his hand up with a smile, laughing.

Daisy laughed nervously. "That's a nice surprise, I thought you would have gone back to your people?"

"I am not needed there as much as I am needed here," he concluded with a smile.

Daisy chuckled to herself. "We are going to need as much help as we can get." Her head tilted to the right.

Murgo stood beside her staring at her intently. "Who are the men?" He didn't take his eyes off Daisy's eyes.

Her fangs receded into her face. "They were originally intending to take over this kingdom, however that is no longer the case."

Murgo glanced at the moon. "The situation we seem to be in is getting more complicated." He reached for her hand and to his surprise she didn't retract it.

Kit left Daisy staring into the night sky. She made her way into the dimly lit hut. She noted as she entered that the princess was huddled next to Bjoarn. She appeared to be twitching slightly. Kit's eyebrows furrowed together, she hoped that the princess was going to pull through. She looked around the room and was amazed at how these complete strangers were looking after each other as if they had known each other for years. She guessed as she sat on her own straw mattress that complete tragedy and the risk to one's life did that to you. Kit tried to settle under the hessian blanket but she couldn't relax. She found herself glancing at the princess thinking she would have to come up with a solution to help Nekite if she were to return to the palace to rule over the people.

Day broke with the tweeting of birds, the sun trying to

penetrate through the hut's darkness not quite achieving it. Dust particles floated through the still dry air. Kit rolled on to her back which made the straw mattress scratch even more. As she tried to move again to relieve the itching, Kit noticed a tattooed arm draped over her. She gave a sideways glance, finding that the arm belonged to Destin, she gave an internal sigh. Thanking her lucky stars it was Destin, and not another one of those men. As she got up, she noticed Daisy snuggled into Murgo which brought a smile to her face. Kit was pleased he had found them, at least they had another person on their side. Today she had decided her and Daisy were to create a battle plan. They knew the castle inside out: knowing all the corridors, secret passages and turrets they should have no problem implementing a plan. Once they had one.

Bjoarn had propped the princess up against the outside of the hut, meaning she could get the full benefit of the sun's warmth. He perched next to her holding an ancient crockery bowl full of gruel, trying to persuade the princess to hold the bone spoon.

"I think she is too far gone, brother." Ethan stood behind them casting shadows over the princess.

"She needs to regain her strength is all," Bjoarn replied through slightly gritted teeth, he knew it didn't look great but he was sure the princess would come round.

Ethan shook his head. "I don't understand you, one minute you're breaking a girl's ribs." He pointed to where the Mage stood chatting intensely to Kit and Daisy. "Then the next minute you are nursing a girl back to health." Ethan paused looking at the princess. "Well at least trying to."

"You don't understand." Bjoarn shook his head slightly. "This girl is Princess Nekite of this kingdom."

Ethan's eyes widened slightly. "Have you told father?" he asked in a hushed whisper.

Bjoarn shook his head. "No, he will expect me to kill her."

Ethan nodded in understanding, their father could be cruel at times.

"Anyway, Father is returning to the boats with his most trusted men. He doesn't want to be a part of this from this point onwards." Bjoarn turned his attention back to the princess.

After trying to get the princess to eat and failing to do so, Bjoarn decided that she needed to bathe as that might refresh her, which would be tricky as he had no doubt the woman in this settlement would have something to say about him trying to do it. He rubbed his hair with his hand absentmindedly.

He decided to speak to Kit first, who was drawing on parchment outside of their hut. "Hello, could you help me for a short period of time, I was going to bathe the princess," he asked, slightly sheepishly.

"I'm sorry, I'm busy right now. I'm sure someone else could help you though," Kit replied without taking her eyes from the parchment.

Bjoarn decided to try Daisy next, who was sitting with her own parchment, but before he had a chance to speak, she flat out refused to help. He didn't want to trouble the revolt members for two reasons: one, they seemed genuinely scared of him, and, secondly, they had their own lives to be getting on with. He sighed as he realised the only option left was the Mage, who always kept her distance from him. He sighed again, he supposed that was due to the rib incident.

He made his way over to where she was sat sharpening arrowheads. He cleared his throat in an attempt to get her attention. When she didn't react, he swallowed hard.

"Hello, I wondered if you had time to help me?" he stuttered out the question. At first the Mage merely blinked, shaking her head in a no motion.

"It wouldn't be helping me, as such, it is the princess. I thought she could do with a bath, it might refresh her," he carried on, regardless of the shaking head.

The Mage stopped sharpening the arrowhead. She glanced over at the tiny frame of the princess then back to this big brute. The thought of him trying to bathe the princess filled her head with horror. She heard herself say, "Yes of course I will help the princess."

The Mage started to warm the water over the fire, her thoughts drifted slightly as she stared into the bubbling water. She had been regarded as an outcast when she arrived back here, no warm welcome, no congratulations for bringing the gods here, no praise, no nothing. The bubbling water swirled round as the heat grew from the fire; Alston hadn't even been to come and see her. She suppressed a sigh. She got a feeling in the pit of her stomach that she was no longer wanted here. She was an outcast.

"I have got the barrel ready, it just needs the water now," Bjoarn said, cutting into her thoughts. "Right, if you watch the water, I will get the princess ready," she replied, not looking at him.

Undressing the princess proved very difficult. She was a dead weight in her catatonic state. Trying to lift her arms proved to be a task in itself; the mage started to sweat a little at the effort of undressing her. The fine silk material soft against her rough weathered hands. The Mage stopped for a second with a frown on her face. She just couldn't understand how to unlace the corset. Her head tilted to the side trying to work it out.

"Do you need help?" Bjoarn asked from where he stood in the doorway. He had been sneaking glances at her with amusement.

The Mage straightened. "How could you help, it's not like you wear one?" The Mage placed her hands on her hips.

Bjoarn cleared his throat. "No, but I have had many experiences taking them off." He laughed, amused as the Mage's face coloured.

The Mage was lost for words for a second then replied, "Fine, just be gentle and don't peek at her," she exclaimed.

"I wouldn't anyway she's not my type," Bjoarn said with a laugh, resulting in the Mage's face colouring further.

The princess was placed in the warm water with Bjoarn facing the back and the Mage doing the cleaning with a rag. The Mage was about to wash the princess's face when she heard a moan-like sound. She leant forward, furrowing her brow, doubting herself that she had heard anything. Then she heard it again.

"Bjoarn, did you hear that?" Excitement filled her voice.

"The moan? I thought that was you," he replied, also leaning forward. The Mage shook her head venomously.

"I thought you were enjoying…" Before he could finish his sentence, the Mage reached round the princess and swatted at him. He dodged away easily.

"Please take this seriously," the Mage replied.

He laughed at her whilst taking a step forward, listening intently to the princess. None of them dared move until the princess moaned again.

They both looked at each other not daring to hope this was a good sign.

"Hello, Princess, it is I, the Mage. I am not sure if you will remember me," she said, gently holding onto her arm.

The princess moved her head in a slow jerky movement to look at the Mage, who smiled encouragingly at her.

"Yes, I remember." The princess croaked, her head slumping forward with the effort.

Chapter Twenty-Two

After not hearing her voice for so long it seemed weird hearing it again. The princess had been moved from the water into the hut, quickly. She sat huddled up in an old hessian blanket staring at the faces in front of her.

"We thought we had lost you there, Princess." Daisy smiled at her.

"Who are these men?" she croaked out the question, looking down to see if her modesty was still intact, the hessian blanket only just managing to cover her.

She tugged at the corners hoping it would help as Kit replied, "They are our new friends. They are here to help us." Nodding her head. Her tone of voice carried an air of authority that no one dared cross.

The princess stopped playing with the hessian blanket and looked briefly round the dark damp hut. "How long are we staying here for?" A little shudder ran through her body.

"I cannot say for certain, your majesty, for as long as needed is my only answer." Kit bent down in front of the princess. "I promise everything will be all right." Kit straightened again looking around the group of people.

The princess nodded slightly in response as everyone but the Mage filed out of the door.

"We will get you some more suitable clothes, you might have to alter them though as they might not fit." The Mage returned with a bundle of rags.

The princess's eyes widened in alarm as she picked the first rag up with an outstretched hand. "Can I not wear my own clothes?" the princess asked, inspecting the rags.

"They are highly unsuitable," the Mage replied.

"I do not know how to alter material," she stuttered, turning the old cloth in her hands.

"I will show you, it is a great skill to have," the Mage replied, beaming with enthusiasm at an old wooden box in between them which was over flowing with thread, needles and scraps of material.

The princess's eyes widened further as the Mage showed her how to thread a needle, how to achieve a simple stitch and how to tie a knot. The princess took the needle to the cloth in a clumsy heavy-handed way. Eventually after many restarts she had something that resembled a long tunic type dress. The princess lifted it up to look at her handiwork, almost laughing when she saw the right sleeve was longer then the left and the hem line going upwards at an angle. She turned it round, feeling the coarse material in her soft delicate hands. The princess felt something almost heavy in her chest. She wondered if it could be pride, at being able to achieve this tunic in such a short space of time. She arched an eyebrow, looking at the material. Even though it wasn't bejewelled or woven in the finest of silks or draped in fur she had done this all by herself. A smile played on her lips.

"What else can you show me?" she enquired in a small but excited voice.

The Mage gave a short laugh before answering, "Do not worry, your majesty, I have lots of skills I can teach you."

The Mage provided her with some small leather boots

instead of the silk slippers the princess had originally worn. The Mage showed her how to perform simple tasks such as how to warm water, how to start gruel in the pot and how to prepare the dinner utensils. The princess inspected the rough pots in her hand, feeling the chips and the cracks; she smiled to herself at how different this was to the silver and gold at the palace.

"May I ask a question?" The Mage interrupted her thoughts from across the hut. "Of course, ask anything." The princess smiled over to the Mage.

"Where were you when we were on this journey?" The Mage cocked her head to the side.

The princess's brow creased with confusion.

"Sorry, that didn't make sense." The Mage laughed at herself. "Let me try again." She took a deep breath. "After we met Murgo, the blue man, you went into a sort of trance as if you weren't really with us, if you understand me." The Mage trailed off.

The princess nodded, her mind travelling back to two days ago where she remembered how she was sat down smiling ineptly, staring into space, as the demons within her head clawed at her threatening to bring the darkness that lurked in the shadows of her mind. As she sat smiling round at her new friends, her protectors, the demons in her head won. They climbed over the wall she had built until they had reached the surface.

"I think there are demons in my head." Her head hung low as the words came out barely a whisper.

Chapter Twenty-Three

Eva pretended to stumble as she hopped on one leg through the villages making her way to the castle. She tried not to smile to herself as this had been far too easy. She heard whispers as she travelled, people wondering if she was the princess, where had she been and what had happened to her, but none of them offering to help which made it even easier. If they didn't get too close, they wouldn't be able to tell if she was the princess, well, not that they had seen much of her anyway Eva mused to herself. She reached the castle gates and screamed for help, placing a thin delicate hand to her forehead before dramatically falling to the ground, and, just as planned, the general of the red devils dressed as a palace guard came rushing to her side to take her into the palace.

The following morning the clouds darkened, the sky menacingly stopped all chances of the sun breaking through, the wind created a cool breeze. Daisy stood over Kit looking at the plans that had been drawn out so far. She cocked her head to the side frowning slightly.

"So let me get this right." Daisy paused for a second. "We are waging war on the kingdom." Daisy looked around at the revolt members rushing around. "With wooden sticks?" Daisy said, almost laughing.

Kit sighed and rubbed her eyes. "I don't like it any more than you but if these Vikings." She pointed towards Destin and his men. "Think they could take down the kingdom without our help they sure can with us."

Daisy placed her hands on her hips, vaguely watching the princess and the Mage trying to sharpen what weapons they had.

"Okay, I understand what you are saying, but you do realise we will have to train these people if we have any chance of succeeding," Daisy said, gazing around the assembly of wooden huts.

Kit stopped scribbling on a piece of parchment. Looking at the peasants gathering wood, cooking and herding animals around she sighed. "Yes, that might take some time which we almost certainly don't have."

Both Kit and Daisy informed the leader of the revolt of their plan of storming the castle. They stood before him in his hut next to the blazing fire which occasionally spat at them. However, Daisy sensed displeasure radiating from him. He disagreed with the shortcomings, loudly voiced his opinion that in his mind his followers were ready to fight which made Daisy openly laugh at him which displeased him even more.

"I can see we disagree on many aspects of this plan. I suggest you listen to me," Kit's claws shot out of her hand which in turn made Daisy's fangs slide from her mouth to her neck. Both of their eyes shone brightly, it was as if they were torches. "You do not have the means to storm the castle as they call it." Kit arched an eyebrow. "You need our help, you requested our help, so I am telling you what will happen." Kit's voice was a chilly calm.

Daisy stood next to her, silently calm and unmoveable. The revolt's leader looked from one to the other in stunned silence before simply muttering the words, "As you wish, do as you see fit." With that he turned round making his cloak swirl.

Once back outside, the cloudy daylight seemed bright compared to the dark hut from which they had emerged. Daisy rubbed her eyes.

"I do not like that man. I think revenge has warped him into an evil twisted being," Daisy stated, flicking her hair and glancing at Kit's raised eyebrow. "He would have sent his followers to their deaths if we weren't able to train them."

Kit looked on into the distance, her mind on the leader who through abuse had turned into the abuser. Her mind briefly wandered into her subconscious of Regeta and the years of abuse she and Daisy had suffered. However, those horrors had not defined them, had not twisted them. They were here to help, not to hurt, it occurred to Kit that Daisy must be right. It was revenge that drove the so-called leader and revenge was a very powerful emotion to harbour. The thought of his people mindlessly following him to their death played on her mind.

"I wonder how many of his people were at the passage when the red devils first struck, it seemed many were slain then." Kit rubbed her temples. "Honestly, what a nightmare."

Daisy looked at her with a half-smile. "Try not to worry, we are here to help them."

Daisy left Kit pondering over the plan as she went to speak to Murgo who she found to be chopping logs, his lean body etched with blue markings, he almost looked mythical with his dark hair. He turned at the sight of her, almost slightly embarrassed, Daisy thought with an internal smile. Murgo put down his axe and smiled on her approach.

"I am splitting logs for arrows, axes and spears," he said

with triumph. "I am glad I can help."

Daisy briefly looked at the ground before speaking softly, "You have done enough for us as it is." She paused. "You have lost a lot of your men." Before she could carry on, she noticed he had closed the gap between them.

Her anxious face looked up to find that Murgo was stood directly in front of her, she could feel his warm breath on her, breathing in steady rhythms. Her body tensed slightly, her hairs on her arms prickled with anticipation and her heartbeat quickened. She almost dared not breathe he was that close to her.

"If you are indeed a god then you are my god," he muttered into her ear.

By the time the sun set and the moon shone bright in the cloudless sky the Mage had taught the princess many a new skill. The princess sat next to the Mage and Bjoarn as they all tucked into more gruel which had been cooked by the princess. Bjoarn dutifully ate the whole lot even though it had a peculiar taste to it. He glanced down at the princess who was pushing the food around the bowl in her hands.

"Are you not hungry?" he asked her.

She startled slightly as if she was deep in thought. "Oh I." She paused. "No, I am not used to this particular food source. I do not think I cooked this well at all" She looked down at her uneaten food in her bowl slightly forlornly.

"For your first time you did great, I ate all mine." He beamed at her.

She smiled meekly at him. She knew that he was just being kind. He interrupted her thoughts by asking, "Are you ready to start training tomorrow?"

She startled for a split second before regaining her composure. "I was not aware I would be required to fight alongside everyone." She looked into his eyes.

He cleared his throat. "I think everyone is needed, your majesty."

She nervously looked around as she wasn't sure who else knew of her identity. She rubbed her arm distractedly.

"Very well," was all she managed to muster.

"Do not worry, your majesty, it is only us that know of your true identity, the secret is safe." He smiled down at her.

The princess sat very still, wondering who actually knew who she was and if she was indeed safe.

The following morning the sun shone bright through the cracked wood which held the hut up, it danced across the floor shining brightly on the princess's face. She hadn't slept well, the faces of her ladies in waiting swimming before her eyes every time she closed them. She got up, changing into the tunic she had created, smoothing out the fabric somewhat proudly. She glanced around the small room at the sleeping figures, however, she noticed the straw mattress that Bjoarn occupied was empty. She opened the door with a creak, her head swivelling to the right then left, her mind noting how still the day was, no wind, no heat, no clouds, nothing. No doubt Kit and Daisy would say it's a perfect day for battle practice. A long loud sigh escaped her mouth.

"No need for that Princess." Bjoarn laughed, coming from the byre.

The princess tried to conceal her surprise. She smiled over at him, brushing a piece of loose hair behind her ear.

"I am ready to start my training." She looked at him straight in the eyes, not quite believing her own ears at what she said.

"I will guide you the best I can." He smiled at her.

Throughout the morning Bjoarn showed the princess how to hold a sword, how to hold a bow and arrow and how to use both. At first the sword felt too heavy and she was clumsy in how she carried it, the handle looked too big, too masculine, in her dainty hands, the metal rough against her soft skin. She kept turning the blade over and over trying to get used to the weight.

Bjoarn's eyebrows furrowed together in puzzlement at the princess jerkily moving the sword around haphazardly. He coughed slightly to get her attention as she seemed in a world of her own as she danced around with the sword.

The princess stopped suddenly, her cheeks reddened. "I got a little carried away," she mumbled to the floor.

Bjoarn laughed at her. "I could see that, let me show you how to hold the sword."

Bjoarn had built a straw man for her to practice sparring. It got off to a slow start with her tripping on her uneven tunic. After that she dropped the sword on her foot which brought tears to eyes; she closed her eyes tight to stop herself sobbing. Bjoarn had to suppress loud sighs as he patiently repeated everything over and over again until the princess was able to successfully aim for the straw man.

Daisy had been watching the princess from afar, occasionally shaking her head in amusement. She knew the princess was trying and really throwing herself into the task which was more than could be said for the revolt members. Daisy turned to see Kit and Destin trying to get the revolt members in an orderly queue to practice formation. However, even that was looking difficult. Daisy watched with utter disbelief, she was grateful she wasn't involved with that today. Daisy and Murgo were going out of the camp for some much-needed supplies as it was pointed out that the grain store was running low. The revolt's leader had made the point very clear, it was due to all the extra mouths he needed to feed. She sighed to herself. She had begun to intensely dislike that man.

The two of them reached the nearest town which had a market in full swing: children clattered around the mud baked tracks, women huddled in groups shrieking and laughing together. Daisy took in the chaotic scene with ease, this was nothing compared to the city where the palace lay but to Murgo it was all slightly overwhelming. Even though he had worn Destin's cloak to cover his blue torso, he felt he stood out from the crowd. He knew he didn't belong in this surrounding. He glanced at Daisy who also wore a hooded cloak and was bobbing and weaving in between people. He tried to keep up with her the best he could. She rounded the corner quickly but abruptly stopped. Murgo crashed into the back of her. Muttering his apologies, he looked up to see the town square awash with people all gathering listening to an official-looking man adorned in the royal emblem. Daisy lifted her finger up to her mouth signalling to keep quiet; they joined the back of the group surrounding the man bellowing out news from a scroll. Murgo glanced at Daisy whose brows furrowed together at what she was hearing.

"This is almost hopeless," Destin said, scratching his head over a bowl of pheasant soup. He gave an audible sigh.

"Yes, I agree this morning didn't go as well as I would have liked," Kit replied, staring off into the distance.

"No wonder we stood no chance against the red devilled

warriors," the Mage said quietly, sat next to Ethan.

The Mage had been a little subdued all morning, the night before she had attempted to talk to Alston which hadn't gone well. She had found him alone in his hut, which at first, she had thought was perfect. However, as soon as she had entered the room the mood became tense and agitated. He had shouted at her over the events of devil's creek insinuating she hadn't helped them. That she had stood and watched them fall. The way in which he had called her an outsider, she winced at the memory. Her thoughts drifted through the argument as it played out in her head. He had suggested that she would have been able to see the warriors coming and had sent their family to their deaths. She gave a little snort at the thought of family. She then shook her head in disbelief, he had seen which way she had sent the eagle, it was opposite to the red devils. She had searched for the gods. She gave a quiet hollow laugh to herself they were definitely not family any more.

"Are you feeling all right?" Ethan asked, worry crept into his voice.

The Mage looked at him dead in the eye. "Yes, just the realisation of people not being what you thought is difficult."

"Ahh, I see, well in that case it is a good thing you have us," he said, smiling broadly, his smile reaching his eyes in genuine happiness.

Her cheeks flushed pink as she looked away, avoiding eye contact, she could feel her heart begin to gallop in her chest.

"We better get on if we have any hope of achieving this over throwing of the king thing." Kit stood up stretching her back.

The small group all followed her to the revolt members clumsily holding sticks all stood in a huddle. Kit let out a loud sigh which Destin fully understood.

The afternoon drew to an end, the sunset casting shadows among the people.

"I think we will end the practice there, thank you for turning up and training with us," Kit shouted to the members so all of them could hear her. She turned to leave as Daisy came running full speed into her almost knocking her off her feet.

"Whoa there, is everything all right?" Kit grasped Daisy's arm in her hand as anxiety filled her face.

Daisy took deep breaths, her chest heaving in and out heavily. "In the town there was a sort of meeting where a palace spokesman declared they had found the princess!" she exclaimed.

At first Kit couldn't understand what she was hearing as she turned to her left where she could see the princess laughing and joking with the others.

"They must have got it wrong." She turned to face Daisy, willing the calm into her voice.

Daisy just shook her head venomously. "They were most certain, it must be Eva continuing with her plan regardless of whether we are alive or not," she said through heavy breaths.

Chapter Twenty-Four

As the darkness fell the despair that filled every inch of Kit felt like a lead weight in her chest, she knew time was running out, that there was only so long they could train for until they had to march towards the palace. The noises of the forest, the rocky mountain area and the sky filled her ears as if it was almost deafening her. She turned away as if she couldn't take the sounds any more. As she turned towards the hut, she knew she wouldn't sleep as the thoughts all jumbled together swimming in front of her eyes.

She had felt panic like this once before, this pure blind panic that you thought would stop the world from going round. She clutched at her chest as her heart quickened, as the memories she had locked away drifted to the surface. She remembered being dragged screaming down a corridor, she remembered trying to fight scratch and crawl her way to freedom. Whatever she tried it wasn't good enough as she was thrown in a white padded room. She ran towards the door which was shut in her face. She shouted and punched the door. Tears rolled down her face in hot large droplets. She remembered how she had screamed until she had lost her voice.

Kit turned away from the memory only to be hit with another memory hidden in the back of her mind. This one was the first time she had seen Daisy with her purple hair and plump figure fighting with an orderly. Kit had stared at this girl who was making as much commotion as she was. They had only made eye contact, for a few seconds, however those few seconds were enough for both girls to connect. After that day they had spoken through the walls of their respective padded cells, sharing everything about their former lives. Kit had found out she had been through a very similar situation where they had both been sold for money. This had united the girls. Kit stared off into the distance as the memory of both girls being dragged through the endless corridors both wide-eyed with dread as they stumbled and tripped. Both girls got pushed through two heavy swing doors, the bright lights causing them to squint. Blinking rapidly, Kit looked around, seeing Daisy being strapped down. Kit surged forward to try and reach out for her friend.

Kit smiled to herself, so much had changed since that day: the relentless beatings, scientific experiments, the pure fear and grief she had felt, the many faces she had met along the way, the many faces she never saw again. She closed her eyes against the memory of all those lost souls. She felt a hand on her arm, she whipped round, eyes bright, claws starting to extend. Destin stood in front of her. A smile spread across her face, the claws instantly retracting.

"It is getting late you should come and rest, we have busy days ahead." He looked at her, concern etched on his face.

She turned back towards the moon. "I have many thoughts. I cannot relax." She sighed heavily.

Destin closed the gap between them. "Let me help you." His eyes looked deep into hers.

Kit couldn't tear her eyes from him, her heartbeat quickened to an almost unbearable pace. She tried to control her breathing. Just as she was sure he was going to kiss her, a loud bang echoed behind them making them both jump apart, flustered to find Bjoarn emptying the fire's ashes out of the door.

The moment was lost as they both stared at Bjoarn clattering around. Kit sighed heavily, not looking at Destin, before heading back to the hut.

After a further two days of training Kit felt the sensation of relief overwhelm her. It almost made her legs give way. The revolt members had gained some skill, they were working in battle formation, learning strength, power and skill. The thought had entered into her mind several times that they might actually have a chance of succeeding at this, even though it might only be a small chance; she smiled to herself sweeping her hair behind her ear. She turned towards the hut that all of them called home for now. Kit spotted the Mage and Ethan sitting very close.

They seemed to be non-stop chatting to one another. It was as if no one else was present in their own world. She tilted her head to the side, smiling as she did so. She carried on watching them from a distance. She watched how animated the Mage looked. She deserved to be happy and Kit seriously hoped this was the beginning of something beautiful for them. This interaction reminded her of the princess and how she was getting on with Bjoarn like a house on fire which did surprise Kit with how he had acted in such a negative manner towards the Mage. Her eyes travelled to where Daisy and Murgo were huddled together, over these two days they hadn't really left each other's side which had meant she had spent more time with Destin. Her heart flickered at the thought of him. She sighed, nothing else had happened between them and she was beginning to think she had imagined it all. Instead of disturbing the group she made her way to the byre to see Puzat. She hopped over the door and sat down quietly in the old straw that littered the floor. Puzat came over, sniffing her hair, which shone silver in the moon light.

Her mind was full of the dramas ahead, but for a split second, she was content with just sitting there on the dirty old straw next to Puzat.

"Where did you spend last night," Daisy asked, a mischievous smile creeping across her face.

Kit handed the revolt member in front of her a spear. "The byre, don't get excited." She laughed at her.

Daisy tutted, turning to grab the heap of bow and arrows to hand out, it was the last day of training and Daisy could sense the air was heavy with nerves, excitement and anticipation. In her opinion they weren't ready for the attack but she knew they had no choice. It had been three days since the news had broken, that the princess had been found. Daisy knew if they were to foil Eva's plans, and return the real princess to the throne, they had no choice but to push forward sooner than they would have liked. Daisy just hoped they weren't too late. If she believed in gods, she would have prayed to them.

Eva lay in the lavish bed, surrounded by silk sheets plumped up goose pillows and rich furs; she let her hand run along the fine fabric almost lazily. She let out a contented sigh and let her head fall back on to the pillow. She let out a giggle which she conceded sounded sinister. She almost had to pinch herself with how well the plan had worked. The royal doctor had been paid handsomely to inform the king and Queen that the princess needed rest and should under no circumstance be disturbed in any way. She then had the guard of the red devils stationed outside her door to ward off any well-wishers. The next part of the plan would be a little trickier. Eva pushed herself out of the enormous bed to walk across the vast room to practice the dark magic she had learnt. She perched herself on the small gold painted stool in front of the polished metal mirror, her reflection staring back at her. It was uncanny how much she looked like the princess and once the magic words were spoken no one would recognise her as Eva again. She grabbed a few glass jars containing Saint John's wart, eye of newt and the feather of a golden eagle. She tilted her head as she looked at the parchment in front of her. There was a fourth ingredient that hadn't yet been retrieved for her. She let out an exasperated sigh. She punched the table. The general had got on her last nerve; she stood up quickly sending the stool flying backwards. She stormed to the door and yanked it open with force.

"Where is the general?" Eva demanded in a haughty manner.

The soldier started composing himself, his eyes darting right and left rapidly. "He has gone for his break, madam," the soldier stuttered.

"When he is back, tell him I need a chatterpie's heart." Eva span around in a split second. "Oh, and it is your majesty from now on." She slammed the door in her wake.

They had left the safety of the revolt's hideout, trekking through the forest the dread filling Daisy and Kit's heart felt heavy within their chests, they rode side by side going over the plans making sure every eventuality was seen too.

"I honestly cannot believe we are doing this," Daisy muttered to Kit.

"No but it feels right don't you think?" Kit didn't take her eyes off the track in front as she spoke.

"I agree this is the right course of action," Daisy replied turning to look at the princess who rode behind with Bjoarn.

The two of them appeared to be chatting away happily enough, he was making small talk as the princess sat upon the scruffy pony with rigid shoulders.

Daisy turned back around. "I hope we all survive this, I have actually begun to like these people." She looked at kit.

"Well, most of them." Kit laughed.

"Definitely not the revolt's leader." Daisy laughed back.

Next to Bjoarn, Ethan and the Mage rode in silence, the Mage's thoughts drifting to the last battle they had engaged in, shaking her head every once in a while, with the great loss they had all suffered. She could feel eyes on the back of her every time she glanced backwards. Alston had been staring at her. His eyes bore into her. She opened her mouth to speak before promptly shutting it.

"I have nothing to say to you apart from your new friends better know what they are doing," he cruelly sneered at her.

The Mage turned back around silently. A tear rolled down her cheek. She knew in her heart Kit and Daisy wouldn't let any of them down. She trusted them with her life.

Ethan reached across from his pony to wipe the tear from her face, she turned to look at him, her face full of sorrow, and the pain she felt was etched across her features. Ethan looked back towards Alston with a scowl, he would have to sort that situation out as he couldn't see the Mage upset like this.

However, it would have to wait, he snorted to himself, that was if they all survived.

Destin rode next to Alston who he noticed stared at the back of the Mage with narrowed dark angry eyes, barely blinking, just staring. Destin kept making side glances at him wondering what the matter with him was.

"That is quite the look you have there," Destin finally remarked in a jovial way.

Destin watched Alston closely for a reaction, his eye twitched slightly and his face coloured a pink hue. However, he didn't mutter a word.

"If I was you, I would stop blaming the Mage for what has transpired and focus all your energy on beating these red devils." His tone was harder than his usual softly spoken tones.

Alston didn't react, just carried on glaring at the back of the Mage.

Murgo raced through the trees grabbing one branch after another, always in front of the group looking for any danger, turning and twisting his head at any noise or sight. He had briefly thought about making a detour to see his clan but deep within his heart he knew he would be regarded as stranger, an outcast, from now on for choosing these people over his own. He, however, had no regrets. He knew that what this group of misfits were about to achieve would go down in history and he had to be a part of it.

They reached the devil's creek within two days. Even though the flood water had washed away all the evidence of what had occurred, the princess couldn't bear it. She couldn't bear the rocky terrain where she had escaped to, she couldn't bear the muddy track which she had shimmed over on her belly under the carriage. She couldn't bear any of it. She closed her eyes tightly, almost not daring to breath. Her body gave involuntary shudders as the scenes she had witnessed on that track played out in her mind.

Bjoarn glanced at her. "Are you quite well your majesty?" he asked, leaning forward out of the saddle to look at her scrunched-up face.

"Yes of course," the princess managed to mutter through clenched teeth, her eyes tightly shut.

Bjoarn stared at the princess for a second before urging his hairy pony forward to catch up with Kit and Daisy. As the pony drew level with Puzat, Bjoarn asked in a muted voice, "The princess won't open her eyes?"

Both of them whipped round to see the princess clutching onto the pony's mane, her shoulders hunched and face screwed up.

Kit frowned before turning back. "I think it will be because her friends were killed here, this place will bring back all those unpleasant memories, let us just hope she doesn't go back into her state of shock," she said quietly.

Daisy mumbled her agreement before turning her attention on the track ahead. "Kit?" she asked, as Bjoarn rejoined the princess.

"Yes Daisy?" she smiled at Daisy knowing that she needed the reassurance they all inevitably needed.

"So let me get this straight, we are going to march on in to the palace grounds, put the princess on the throne and just walk out?" Daisy asked with an arched eyebrow and tilted head.

Kit laughed. "Yes, just like that, it seems pretty simple don't you agree?" A smile played on Kit's lips.

"I agree, I cannot see what would go wrong." Daisy laughed sarcastically back. She gathered the reins to Demon and pushed forward into a rhythmic canter.

The group cantered through the creek as quickly as they dared, the thought that red devil spies may be lying in wait for them had sat heavily in Kit's mind. However, as the group followed the well-worn track which led towards the city which surrounded the palace, the thought began to fade.

"We are going to attract some attention once in the city walls," Daisy shouted over to Kit who nodded back.

Her claws shot from her hands, as if on cue, she gave a side glance towards Daisy whose fangs hung past her chin. Kit sighed, they could both feel the air heavy with tension as if the city and the palace knew what was about to take place. The clouds darkened as if on cue, the tension building around them filling their ears.

Eva sprang up with a jolt that wrenched her neck. She placed her hand on it tenderly, frowning as she did so, turning to the door where she heard an urgent thudding.

"Who is it?" Eva demanded, her voice laced with irritation.

"The general," a hushed frantic voice replied.

Eva sighed and rolled her eyes before letting the man into her lavish room.

"Please be careful where you stand. I do not want the room becoming untidy," she drawled at him.

"Your Majesty, I have grave news." He paused for a second while she motioned for him to carry on. "The gods have formed an army and are marching towards the palace as we speak." His voice trailed off. His eyes avoided her face.

For a moment Eva was speechless. She couldn't form words. The rational side of her brain knew this would happen at some point but she had hoped her plan would have been in place and she would have all the ingredients for the spell. The spell was of dark, dark, magic: the sort of magic you get told exists but you never witness it or believe it. But Eva had grown up with this witchcraft, it was in her blood coursing through her veins. This certain spell she so badly needed would make anyone looking at her think it was indeed the princess they were addressing. However, the problem was she had not achieved this yet due to not having all the components. She cursed the red devil's incompetence for gathering her ingredients.

"Well, I suggest you get the red warriors together," Eva managed to meekly reply, "I want this squashing."

Tilting her head towards the door finishing the conversation there, once the general had left the room, she walked over to the narrow window trying to crane her neck towards the city to catch a glimpse of the approaching army.

Chapter Twenty-Five

Kit and Daisy led the way through the huge gates, both of them bracing themselves as they watched people suddenly stop in the street staring up at them, eyes wide with shock. Silence descended which felt like time had stopped. The horses skidded to a halt, dirt and gravel flew into the air and Puzat let out a snort which broke the trance. People started scurrying around, running through doors, dropping baskets full of fruit and vegetables. An apple rolled across the dirt track stopping just before Puzat.

"We need to keep moving," Daisy shouted over the chaos surrounding them.

They urged the ponies on through the swarm of panicked peasants and noble people who were screaming and dashing in between the group. As they rounded the corner Kit glimpsed a flash of red.

"Archers are you ready?" She turned, shouting towards the revolt members who clutched the bows to their chest. They nodded back, white with terror, eyes wide.

"Destin?" Kit shouted.

"Yes!" he replied, trying to control the startled horse beneath him.

"Take your men to the left at this next junction, we need to split the red warriors up." She tried to smile at him, creating reassurance, but not quite pulling it off.

The group pushed on in to a canter. The cantering ponies filled the tiny streets of the city, the sound of the hooves echoing around them. The streets were so narrow their knees grazed on the rough walls of the crudely built buildings. Every turn that Kit made she saw a flash of red. Her heart rate began to quicken. It seemed they were in every street, every house and every corner. As they rounded another corner Kit pulled up Puzat quickly, he skidded, before rearing and turning at the sight of a group of red warriors. Daisy struggled to gain control of Demon who was striking out at the red warriors. The men's masks showed no emotion as they twisted their necks up towards the sky; Kit followed their gaze to find other red warriors armed with arrows looking down upon them. She glanced towards Daisy who was staring at one red warrior in particular. It appeared she was fixated on him, her eyes never moving from the mask, watching his every movement.

"Daisy snap out of it," Kit whispered loudly.

Daisy couldn't tear her eyes away from the man who she knew very well, she could have picked him out of any group of men, mask or not, as they had been lovers after all.

Daisy smiled with anger in her eyes. "I spy with my eye the general of the palace guards," she spat out.

Kit glanced in the direction of the man who carried a palace sword, she swallowed hard, it dawned on Kit this had gotten really big and for the first time, fear gripped her heart at the thought they may not be able to pull this off. They were seriously outnumbered and out-skilled. Eva had got the palace guards under her thumb working for her, doing her dirty work; she just hoped that Destin, the princess and his men were having better luck then them.

The Mage yanked at her pony's mouth, spinning it around

ready to canter in the direction they had come, to find they were blocked by yet more red warriors. Flustered, the Mage felt her heart beat quicken to an incredible speed, she was certain they could see it through her clothes. She glanced over to Kit and Daisy who looked calm and collected which reassured her they would get out of this. She grabbed her bow and arrow, aiming for the rooftop warriors, her eyes squinting against the sky. She knew she couldn't miss. Out of the corner of her eye she saw Kit jump off Puzat in an effortless somersault landing crouched low to the floor chanting. The wind intensified, almost knocking the Mage off the pony, suddenly the ground shook with such force the roof timbers fell to the floor, doors slammed and windows creaked. The Mage's eyes widened as she heard Kit say "If they want gods let us show them gods."

The Mage tried to concentrate on aiming her arrow at the red warriors on the rooftops who were stumbling about, some slipped on falling roof timbers but she couldn't keep her eyes off Kit who was etching in the ground with her claws fully extended odd ancient symbols. The clouds darkened further as if it was the middle of the night, the wind wiped through the streets, swirling around them ruffling the manes and tails of the ponies who had begun to snort in panic. There was a sudden chill in the air causing goose bumps to run all along the Mage's arms, if she hadn't been holding her bow and arrow she would have clutched at her sides for warmth. As Kit stood, the ground let out an incredible noise, a huge booming noise an almost crashing sound echoed around the now silent streets.

The world stood still for a split second. People moved in slow motion, the trees stopped moving, the wind stopped, the dust settled when suddenly the cobbles cracked open, gaping

159

as the crack grew and grew in size almost separating the cobbled road in half. The Mage heard herself shriek in terror as a skeletal hand shot out of the gaping crack, the rotting flesh that hung loosely to the bone filled her nostrils. Then another hand clawed its way out of the hole scraping at the loose cobbles above, it pulled clumps of earth away from the edges as a forearm appeared then the top of a skull appeared shiny bright against the sky. The rotting skeletal figure dragged itself through the gap as it stood upright, teeth drawn back behind the almost non-existent lips. Tattered fabric hung slackly from the shoulder blades, moth eaten and bedraggled, adorned with rusty weapons in scabbards that were stained with years' worth of mud.

The Mage clutched at the pony's mane in comfort as one after another of these figures rose from the fiery depths of the underworld. She tore her eyes from the scene playing out in front of her to steal a glance at the other revolt members, Alston's face was sheet white with a tinge of green as if he were about to vomit. The Mage let out a snort. She felt a small bubble of hatred for him rise within her, before she looked away, he caught her watching him, his eyes were large round and frightened. Something clicked within her, an internal knowing that nothing would ever be the same again. She knew she would never help him or the revolt members again. Her duty was to Kit, Daisy and most importantly the princess.

The revolt's leader thought this whole battle was to get him into power, to get him on the throne. As the Mage aimed her arrow at the red warrior upon the roof, she wasn't doing it for him or the members, but for the princess and her throne.

Kit felt Daisy jump down and join her chanting repeatedly getting louder and louder, Kit turned to face Daisy smiling.

Daisy nodded back knowing they would need a sacrifice for the army of the dead to fight alongside them.

Kit turned, eyes bright, towards the Mage who still clutched her bow and arrow. Kit slightly turned her vision towards the stumbling rooftop red warriors mouthing shoot one. Kit turned back to the rising dead army; Daisy never stopped chanting beside her. Kit spoke to the skeletal figures before them. Her ancient tones floated above the wind whilst the red warriors' eyes widened with shock and terror.

"Hello my friends, we meet again. I am afraid I need more help," Kit spoke softly at the skeletal army.

With shaking hands, the Mage raised her arm higher, looking directly at the rooftop.

Her arm shook with the effort of holding her bow up, she closed one eye, held her breath and fired. A second went by then a thud as the body crumpled in a heap on the floor. In a swift movement, Kit jumped over and plunged her claws into the warrior's chest, ripping his heart out in one fluid motion. Kit walked over to the gaping crack that seared through the cobbled streets; she dropped the once-beating heart into the fiery depths of the underworld. The flames roared skyward causing unbearable heat; the Mage covered her eyes, the heat stinging them.

The eyes of the walking dead grew bright with blues and purples. The undead raised their rusty weapons to the darkening sky yelling in all languages known to man.

The walking dead surged forward, a loud growl almost grumble escaping their mouths. The Mage felt the skeletal figures push past her almost knocking her off the scruffy squat pony. Her heartbeats urged, as the red warriors sprang into action, she raised her bow and arrow again, took a deep breath, and fired.

Kit sprung over the first line of warriors landing in a somersault low to the floor, springing up, slashing away the swords pointed in her direction. Daisy ducked and dodged around the rearing horses ending up by Kit's side, blood already dripping from her fangs as she left a pile of warriors in her wake. A big droplet of blood hit the floor with a splat as Daisy's breath came in short sharp rasps.

"You cannot scare us with your little tricks and games," shouted the red warrior general, looking Daisy right in the eye.

"I wish this was a game, sweetie," drawled Daisy with an added flick of her hair.

"I will cut your tongue out as a trophy," he shouted through gritted teeth.

Daisy waggled her tongue at him with an arched eyebrow mocking him even more, a smirk crept across Kit's face and she stamped the floor heavily with her right foot creating further shockwaves through the ground.

"I love how you make friends so effortlessly." Kit openly laughed at Daisy's display.

"I love the attention," Daisy smirked back as a foolish red warrior ran past the general with his sword drawn, making a beeline for Daisy.

Daisy effortlessly stepped to the right, rotating her shoulder slightly as she did so she could lean forward and sink her teeth into the unsuspecting neck of the warrior. The sound of flesh ripping apart, crunching cartilage, then finally the snapping of bones. Daisy let the limp body fall to the floor, wiping the blood off with the back of her hand, she stretched her neck smiling a bloody grin.

Chapter Twenty-Six

The army of the dead rushed past Kit and Daisy, striking out as the red warriors drew their weapons, also surging forward. The streets echoed with the clash of swords, the groans from fallen men, shouting and swearing from both sides.

The Mage fired arrows one after another, barely having time to take a breath, sweat rolled down her forehead. An arrow came whizzing past inches away from her shoulder. She let out a terrified scream. Before she could collect her thoughts, she was knocked from her pony onto the ground. She felt the wind leave her body momentarily, her ribs ached, landing heavily on her side her eyes watered, stinging her face. After a few seconds her sight came into focus, she could see dancing hooves all around her. She rolled away from the prancing hooves, narrowly missing being landed on. She rolled over, pushing herself up, when suddenly she felt a huge pain in her back, sagging to the floor as the pain swept over her in huge waves. A tear ran down her check as she took deep ragged breaths before reaching for her bow and arrow. The red warrior who had struck her held a huge mace with iron spikes encasing it; the warrior turned his head to the side, the mask upon his face smirking down on her. The Mage tried to aim her arrow at him but with one swift movement he kicked it out of her hand. She shuffled backwards as fast as she could manage, dragging her body through the street. As fast as she shuffled, his pace matched. He ducked under swinging swords, wrung the neck of a nearby undead warrior, never missing a beat, his eyes fixed upon hers with every movement getting closer and closer to the Mage.

She shuffled backwards until she hit a building wall. Her eyes widened as the hard wooden building pressed into her back; she glanced upwards towards the building's roof and let out a little gasp of terror. She turned to face the oncoming onslaught. She held her breath, scrunched her eyes shut and waited for the inevitable. Suddenly she felt a drop hit her forehead. Her eyes lifted to find Kit's claws through the warrior's chest, blood splattered the wall behind her. With her free hand, Kit helped the Mage up. The deep red blood ran down the wall creating a startling contrast to the Mage's white face as she stared at the waterfall effect the blood was making.

"You are doing great, we are getting there." She smiled and disappeared into the throng of people within an instant.

The Mage tore her eyes from the wall, picking her bow and arrow up, wincing in pain. Her hand went to her back, where the mace had struck her, she could feel grazes, bumps and lumps, she let out a relieved sigh. It seemed she had gotten this far without serious injury, she knew she couldn't quit now, raising her arrow she once again fired it at the enemy.

Daisy ripped apart another warrior's throat and span around throwing an axe into the back of another; she drew a deep breath as she watched the two men fall to the floor within seconds of each other. She retrieved the axe with a spring in her step before coming to a screeching halt as she came face to face with the general of the guards. Her lover. She blinked rapidly before arching an eyebrow.

"Fancy meeting you here," she drawled at him with a nasty smile written on her face.

He laughed at her. "It is my job to defend the royal family, palace and kingdom from our enemies," he spat at her.

She reached for her sword from within the scabbard pointing it towards the guards general. "I'll remember that we're enemies next time you're knocking on my chamber door."

The two swords clashed together as he launched at her, Daisy deflected the advance with ease, sidestepping around and kicking him over. As he lay on the ground, she went to strike him, he quickly held his sword up, the two swords clashing.

"You won't win," he said through gritted teeth.

Daisy took the pressure off his sword allowing him to stand upright. "You do not even know what or who you are fighting for." She spun around, swords clashing once again.

The two of them struggled through the street, neither one of them letting up. A sweat bead dropped from Daisy's forehead. The two of them ducked, dived and dodged each other among the mass of the two fighting sides.

"I never liked you anyway," the general snarled at her as he too was trying to catch his breath.

Daisy snorted softly as she looked upon the many dead bodies strewn around the street, the faces of many revolt members staring unblinking, unseeing, at her.

"Try not to tell lies it is not very becoming of you," she hit back.

Daisy straightened her spine and ran at him. She punched him straight in the nose, bone crunching under her fist, followed by a knee to his groin area. The general crumpled to the floor.

"I think your time is up here, I also think my sword is too good for you." She kicked his hands away causing his bloody nose to fall to the ground.

"You think you are the best, you think you are untouchable because you are the general. Well, guess what, you are just like any one of us, you are mortal." She kicked his body over so he was lying on his back in a huddle. She landed punch after punch, releasing all the anger she had stored up.

Kit backflipped to avoid another arrow. She crouched low to the floor scanning the legs of the surrounding people looking for Daisy. Her brows came together as she eventually saw Daisy sat above a man landing heavy punches upon him. Kit rolled under a panicked pony to get a closer look at what Daisy was doing. She watched as Daisy straightened herself up, picking a sword up, looking directly into the eyes of the man who used to be her beloved general, the eyes that stared back were full of hatred, small black venomous beads set deep into his face. Daisy pulled back and without any hesitation plunged the sword into his chest.

Kit managed to reach Daisy before she fell to the ground with exhaustion; she dragged her friend into a door way away from the fighting masses around them.

"I just killed him, Kit, I killed him." Daisy let her head rest on Kit's chest.

"I know, sweetie, I saw." She placed a hand on Daisy's head trying to comfort her.

Daisy pulled away after a few seconds, pulled her shoulders back, let out a sigh and reached for her sword. "Right, let's do this."

She marched off into the heaving group of clashing swords, spikes and maces.

Chapter Twenty-Seven

Eva stormed through the palace hallways; servants cowered in the corners as she barked orders at them to get out of her way. She reached an unused part of the palace where cobwebs hung like curtains, the dark engulfed you and the silence amplified every movement. She skipped down the back stone steps to a rickety ancient door which was near on impossible to move due to being unused for many years. She placed her forehead on the cool wood for a second collecting her breath. She braced her shoulder and pushed as hard as she could, the door let out a loud groan as if protesting. The door opened with a juddering movement. The morning breeze flittered around her, the smell of sweat quickly filled her nose. She pulled back in disgust, the red warrior general stood before her. The blood that covered his face had seeped into the wrinkles that lined his face; Eva turned her head slightly to the right examining his face. He seemed to have aged a lot, since the last time she had seen him. He stood wearily, dark circles around his eyes, cuts and grazes over his hands, face and arms.

"Any news, have you retrieved my last item?" Eva said, tapping her foot on the ground in impatience.

"My lady, we are losing on the east side of the palace, they have too many soldiers, I don't have men available to retrieve the item in question." The general stared at Eva straight in her eyes not avoiding her glare.

"What about the west side?" she demanded, hands on hips.

"They are holding their own but for how long I am unable to say." His gaze remained steady, almost daring her to challenge him.

Eva let out a loud sigh. "How peasants can beat the best in the business confuses me," she barely hid her snarl.

The general stood in front of Eva for a second before turning away. "I have to go and stop this endless slaughter, you will not win this."

"It's your majesty!" she screamed after him.

Eva stared at the man's back as he walked away. She couldn't believe the audacity of this man. How dare he walk away and how dare he say he would stop this.

She ran back up the stairs as quickly as she could without tripping on the dainty silk slippers, her mind raced with what she could do to stop this falling down around her.

The general walked away, heading through the narrow streets towards the sound of screaming, shouting and groaning. His pace was slow, reluctant to travel further into the mess before him.

He paused for a moment surveying the scene, men clutched at wounds, some lay on the floor gasping in disbelief but most lay open-eyed having taken their last breath.

He stood behind a wall which had half fallen down in the commotion. He watched from his hidden spot the two gods jumping, spinning and slashing anyone that crossed their path. He was entranced with their grace and elegance. He knew the red warriors couldn't win this battle or even this war. He had witnessed the white-haired god raise the dead, used the ground to her advantage. His men had nothing in comparison. His shoulders slumped slightly. He saw the purple-haired god viciously attacking a soldier, not wasting a second landing her punches. He knew he should join his men but his feet were glued to the ground. His breath quickened as the white-haired god caught sight of him, making her way slowly but surely towards where he was stood. His mind raced, he knew he should move but his feet were firmly rooted to the spot. He watched as she weaved herself in and out of the many still fighting warriors, her long claws glinting in the day light almost blinding him. He placed a hand over his eyes to shield them and within minutes felt the presence of another being, his breath quickened to an almost unbearable amount.

"To your right," Destin shouted over to Bjoarn, who had left himself wide open to attack from the right.

Bjoarn managed to twist around, deflecting the incoming axe with a swat from his arm, making it look effortless and easy. Destin let out a sigh of relief before he dropped to the ground, somersaulted under two fighting soldiers, springing up with ease and planting an axe in the back of the enemy. For a moment Destin glanced around the street, it appeared no one was winning at the moment but he needed to get the princess to the palace quickly.

The wind picked up around them, the smell of death filled his nostrils. "Bjoarn, can you hold the fort?" he shouted across the men.

His older brother slit the throat of yet another warrior whilst nodding viciously over to Destin. Destin ran past several warriors dodging around them. Pushing open a store door where the princess was in hiding, he found her cowered behind a barrel wrapped in a dirty sheet guarded by Murgo.

"Your majesty, we are going to get you into the palace now," he spoke softly but urgently.

Murgo collected up his weapons then helped the princess up. Her eyes were wide, her skin pale, having lost its entire colour through fear. She slotted in behind Destin with Murgo following behind, holding her breath with nerves, not daring to look up, just watching her feet take one step at a time. They headed down a small narrow passage travelling further away from the noise of the battle. They turned right at a junction heading down another narrower passageway. They reached the palace walls with no problems. Destin threw one hook which was attached to a rope up and over the huge wall, he then proceeded to throw the princess over his shoulder with ease. He grabbed the rope between his hands whilst using his feet to help him pull himself up.

Murgo followed him, the rope digging into Destin's hands causing a burning sensation, his face popped over the wall glancing left and right making sure the coast was clear. He tumbled over the wall making sure not to fall on the princess. Murgo leapt gracefully over laughing lightly at him.

"You made that look a lot easier than I did," Destin ruefully said.

Murgo crouched low to the floor, squatting on all fours, glancing in all directions to see if they had been spotted. The princess leant against the rough stone wall catching her breath. This wasn't the easiest way to gain entry into the palace but at least they had got this far.

"We need to be careful, we can't get spotted now," he spoke in a hushed voice.

The princess nodded at him, her hand absent-mindedly running down the rough stone feeling every crevice and crook.

Destin followed Murgo's gaze around the palace walls. "Do you not think it is strange that there are no guards or soldiers around protecting the palace?" he whispered.

"I must admit I was expecting to come into contact with guards on these walls, perhaps they have deployed all their men to the streets," Murgo whispered back, as they made their way towards the wooden door crouched low to the wall.

"We must be careful in case this is a trap and they are in fact waiting for us," Destin replied, as he gently pushed the wooden door open, sword at the ready.

Destin ran through darkened corridors with the princess and Murgo following, his unease growing with every corner passed. It just seemed too quiet, eerily quiet. He came to a sudden halt which almost sent the princess crashing into the back of him. His eyes narrowed as he heard a faint creak in the distance. He motioned to the other two to get near the wall as he crouched low. The candle sticks which lit the dim corridor flickered slightly, creating shadows which danced across the stone floor. The shadows were long and menacing. Destin strained to hear the creak again.

Chapter Twenty-Eight

Kit stood in front of the red warrior general lifting her hand to his face. He recoiled in fright. Kit let out a gentle laugh.

"A brave man like you surely can't be scared of someone like me." Kit arched her eyebrows, smiling sweetly at him.

He began stuttering a response when she ripped the devil's mask from his face; he jumped in surprise at the sudden movement.

"Now isn't that better, we can get to know each other better." She smiled with her head tilted to the right.

Daisy straightened up, her eyes shining bright, her heart beating fast in her chest. Carnage lay around her, and she looked back across to the general's body. The blood ran from it as if trying to escape. She watched it pool together. She stared for a few seconds lost in thought. All the memories she had shared with that man running through her mind. The first moment she had met him stuck, though it was one of her fondest memories of him. She remembered she had been thrown through a door on to a muddy uneven floor, her hands splayed out before her. She looked up to see an older gentleman in a uniform she knew belonged to the palace guards, she and Kit had learnt to hate these men working in the whorehouse.

"Where is my friend?" she asked, straightening up, looking directly at the man.

Before answering he walked towards her, grabbing her cheeks in between his right hand's thumb and forefinger. He wasn't scared of her, he didn't back away from her. She smiled widely at him, a twinkle in her eyes. He let go of her face, offering a hand so she could stand.

"We have enlisted you as soldiers, you will start training tomorrow," he stated, but not in an unkind way.

She blinked rapidly at him not quite understanding the situation. "Aren't we free people here?" she managed to say with utter disbelief written across her face.

"I am afraid with your..." He paused for a brief second. "Let's say talents like yours are needed for our army to protect the king at all cost."

She blinked back, rapidly processing the information. He took a step towards her, she didn't recoil. Her gaze was steady on his face memorising every inch, every line, wrinkle and pigment of his skin.

When suddenly a loud crashing banging noise echoed around the room, she snapped her head to the right. She heard Kit screaming, shouting and behaving like a wild animal. She turned to face the man she would later learn was the general of the palace guards, she looked deep into his eyes.

"I do hope you cooperate more than your friend, I would very much like to get to know you better." He didn't take his eyes off her as he spoke.

She nodded back in response as the crashing from the next room echoed around them.

Her eyes swam with tears as the memory played out before her. She tore her eyes away from the body and the memories that surrounded it. She shook her head to try and erase them.

Daisy turned back to the scene in front of her. She saw men crawl in desperation with fatal wounds, the blood trailing behind them. She heard the cries, wailing and agony radiating from the fallen. Men lay motionless, covered in blood, crows circled overhead, squawking menacingly, they had defeated this section of Eva's army with ease, but at such a cost. She glanced around at all the senseless killing almost in awe or shock, she couldn't decide what her feelings were.

"We move to the east side," Daisy shouted to the rest of their men, raising her sword in the air.

Kit looked deep into the red warrior's eyes, his wrinkles, his blood splattered skin. She took in every detail as her eyes swept across his face, not once blinking.

"Get on with it then," he stammered quietly at her.

She snorted slightly. "I don't want to kill you! I actually want you on our side." She flashed him a smile.

"Do you think I would join you after seeing you slaughter my men?" He almost laughed back at her.

Kit simply shrugged her shoulders. "We both don't want Eva to win this." She paused for a second. "I have seen inside your soul, General, this isn't who you are."

"You wouldn't know who I am. Only I know that." He raised his voice, panic inching its way into him. Kit sighed at him, moving around him in a circle. "We all know you don't want to fight any more." she raised her claws and stroked the side of his face, he shot back, flinching away from the sharp talons.

She walked down the narrow passage towards the east street where the rest of the revolt members were fighting.

The red warrior general let his devil mask fall to the floor when he felt a jolt to his shoulder as he was barged past, almost knocking him off his feet; he rebalanced himself to find the other god-like creature starring unblinking into his eyes.

"If you can't beat them, you might as well join them." Daisy laughed at him whilst turning to follow Kit down the passageway.

He stared after them for a second, weighing up which path to follow. He jogged to catch up with them.

They reached the edge of where the Vikings were in full battle mode, they were slaughtering the red warriors, they had gained an advantage once the general had left to speak to Eva, it was as if they had lost their will to fight.

The general looked at the mass of dead soldiers, his soldiers, and let out a stifled cry. He knew in his heart he should have stopped this happening a long time ago. He followed Kit and Daisy as they weaved through the crowd of people almost numb from the experience. He kept his eyes down so as not to upset him further, not looking up at the surrounding scenes as he followed the two gods. They reached the stone wall where there were two ropes swinging gently in the gentle breeze that had begun to stir around them.

"I was thinking you could help us, we are going to find Eva and undo everything she has done." Kit looked at him with a smile.

All the general could manage was a nod.

"Also, we might kill the king." Daisy laughed, flicking her purple hair over her shoulder.

His eyes widened as it had never occurred to him that these creatures might have their own agenda. Before he could respond, Daisy grabbed one rope, tugging at it firmly. "I hope this holds me." She furrowed her eyebrows.

"If it can hold the men it can hold you." Kit laughed.

The general couldn't stop staring at them, their juvenile manner confused him. They were at war and it was if they didn't have a care in the world.

He watched as Kit effortlessly climbed the wall without a rope, using her claws to hoist her way up, he reached for the free rope, his hand shaking slightly.

"We are not that bad I promise." Daisy's tone softened.

The general looked into her deep purple pools of eyes. "I'm hoping you can stop Eva."

"We are not called gods for nothing." Daisy smiled before pulling herself up the rope.

As he strained to hear the sound of another creak, his breath faltered as he kept his gaze steady on the staircase in the distance. A shadow lengthened then danced before turning black, and then one after another the candles flickered and burnt out, blackness descended on them.

The princess felt the hairs on the back of her neck bristle. She grabbed Destin's arm, it felt hard, rigid and tense. She could feel the tension building around them, almost suffocating them, with her free hand she went to touch the dagger that hung from her girdle. The cold steel pressed into her palm comforting her. The seconds that passed felt like hours.

"Do you really think that you two and the little princess could stop me?" the almost growl-like voice came from the stairwell.

The three of them jumped slightly.

The static tension around the princess fizzed and cracked. "Good always overcomes evil, Eva." The princess's voice sounded strong even though she was shaking.

Eva took another step towards them, just one candle illuminated her with an orange fiery look, her footsteps echoing around the silent corridor.

The princess's heartbeat increased, she thought surely Eva could see it jumping out of her chest, a slight chill ran up her body as Eva smiled wickedly in her direction. The princess gripped Destin's arm harder, her finger nails digging into the flesh.

"Eva, we have won the battle outside. You have nowhere to go, please stop this." She paused. "We were friends," the princess pleaded.

"I am afraid, Princess, you don't quite understand, you see if I were to marry Prince Geoffrey, I would have control over Carak and this kingdom, then it's just a matter of time before I conquer more kingdoms." Eva looked down at the gold shimmering dress that adorned her. "But there is a problem I am not a princess." She tilted her head to the right with a raised eyebrow.

The princess opened her mouth then closed it in utter astonishment at the absurd notion of what she was hearing.

"There is a simple solution though." Eva giggled, taking another step forward. "I simply become you, we already have similar features, so Prince Geoffrey wouldn't realise. Let's face it men don't notice anything." She laughed louder.

The princess gulped, her finger nails drawing blood from Destin's arm she had such a tight grip. "That is insane, you cannot possibly think that would work," the princess stuttered.

"An old family spell would help fool your parents, it would have been so simple." Eva paused. "But you just wouldn't die."

The pressure surrounding the princess suddenly popped.

"I guess I will have to do the job myself." She paused again, looking distracted "I'll give you some advice, never let a man do a woman's job." The snarl spread from one corner of her mouth to the other.

Kit stood on the castle's wall, hands on hips, scanning the surroundings; the wind picked up, blowing her hair away from her eyes. She felt a spit of rain hit her shoulder. Kit looked up at the darkening clouds, the sky looked black and angry, in the distance she heard the roll of thunder. Like the time in devil's creek the earth was going to cleanse itself of the bloodshed.

"I am surprised there aren't any guards," Daisy cut into Kit's thoughts as she helped the red warrior general off the rough wall.

"Eva has them hidden in the castle waiting for orders, some are even guarding the king and Queen's chambers keeping them hostage," the general let his head hang low.

"Don't worry, this will be over soon," Kit said, striding towards the wooden door, her claws fully extended ready.

"I suggest you go look for your men and tell them to stand down," Daisy said to the red warrior general.

He nodded back at her and reached for his sword.

Even though the princess knew this was dangerous she took a step forward closing that gap between herself and Eva, the silver dagger glinted in the dim light. Destin rushed forward, edging past her with his sword ready, when suddenly out of nowhere he was knocked off his feet, landing heavily on his right shoulder. The princess let out a scream as a man cloaked in black jumped on Destin.

The scream bounced off the stone walls as Murgo stood in front of the princess, his axe in his hand, ancient protection chants coming from his mouth. The candles all around them grew brighter, almost blinding bright, before they extinguished to total blackness.

Another scream filled the air. The princess felt a sharp, burning, stabbing sensation in her side. Her hand automatically went to her side, it came away sticky and wet, her breath caught in her throat. Tears sprung to her eyes, her other hand had grasped the wall to steady herself as a wave of nausea hit her. The world around her span, she stared at the rough flagstones underneath her feet.

Murgo ran towards the princess, trying to grab her before she fell, however the pitch-black corridor played tricks on his eyes. He tripped on the uneven floor, crashing to his knees. He tried to stand but was knocked over, hitting the floor heavily, he rolled onto his back thrashing his legs wildly.

Chapter Twenty-Nine

The princess crumpled to the floor, her knees hitting the ground with a thud, tears rolled down her cheek in fat droplets. She gasped for breath trying to call out for Murgo.

Murgo rolled over in an attempt to crawl over to the princess. He kicked at the cloaked figure, momentarily unbalancing the enemy. He kicked out again, this time his foot connected with the assailant's head. The assailant fell to the floor groaning in pain. Murgo closed the gap between him and the princess, just as he reached out for her, his legs got dragged from underneath him, his stomach scraping along the stone floor. He let out a groan, his fingers holding onto the edges of the flagstone as he was dragged.

Destin felt another punch land on his cheek, his head bouncing off the floor., Thoughts whirled around his mind: he knew he had to save the princess, but as punch after punch rained down on him, his concentration started to slip, his eyes started to blur, his hearing became muffled, his head fell to the side and he caught a glimpse of an unearthly bright blue light travelling towards them. The blue light grew brighter, it was so intense Destin shielded his eyes with his hand as his head lolled to the side.

In an instant the black-cloaked guy dropped to the floor opposite Destin, a thin line of blood trickled from his mouth dripping to the floor, creating a small pool near the man's shoulder. Before he could react, the sensation of being dragged to his feet hit him, he stared into the bright blue eyes of Kit who smiled at him.

"They almost got you there," a slight worried tone crept into her voice which she shook off. She held onto him until his head stopped spinning and he was steady on his feet.

He looked around to see Daisy straddling and restraining another hooded figure on the ground. Murgo had also gotten to his feet and appeared to be searching for the princess.

"Where is she?" The panic had crept into Murgo's voice, he rapidly glanced around.

"Eva has her," Daisy breathlessly said, she turned her attention back to the hooded figure in her grasp.

"Where is she taking the princess?" Daisy demanded in a low growl, holding the black cloak tighter in her fist.

Blood spluttered out of the man's mouth as he tried to mumble a reply. Daisy shook him hard, his shoulders slumping together heavily. She let him fall to the floor before she asked him again.

"To her chamber, the chamber." The cloaked man's mouth fell open as a bubble of blood formed. Daisy let the man's body hit the floor.

She walked away, worry etched across her face; she headed down the corridor towards what used to be the princess's chamber. Every source of light had been extinguished, but the shadows followed her climbing up the walls, running along the stone floor reaching out to her. Murgo held Destin up as they limped after the girls. The droplets of blood that had fallen from the princess shined from the light radiating from Kit and Daisy.

"Don't lose yourself," Kit called to Daisy as the shadows

swirled around her.

The darkness circled around them, daring them, provoking them, even enticing them to follow where the black mist crept from as it seeped through the cracks of the floor riding up around them cutting Murgo and Destin off from the girls. Destin felt tiny little needle-like claws scraping at his legs, the needle like sensation ran up his legs, the pin pricks creating a small scream.

Kit grabbed for Daisy's hand as the dark mist enveloped them, however, as she did so she found nothing but air, empty, empty, air.

"Daisy!" she called out, trying with everything she had to not let the worry she felt within her lace her words.

Silence echoed back.

Kit spun around, panic bubbling, rising within her, infiltrating her brain. She willed herself calm, she knew she had to keep herself together if they had any chance of getting out of this.

She called out again, "Daisy!" Yet again silence replied.

Then suddenly she felt something rush past her to the left, startled she span around, then yet again another presence rushed past her to the right.

The dark mist thickened, rising faster from the flagstone to the ceiling, it swirled around her, encasing her, suffocating her. Kit ran forward as fast as she could, trying to race through the mist. However, it followed, seeping out of every crack, every crevice it could find. As she ran, faces loomed at her, faces of past acquaintances, family members she hadn't seen in years, people of a time she no longer belonged in.

She called out for Daisy several times, her voice going slightly hoarse, but only silence echoed back.

A tall figure appeared. Kit abruptly came to a halt, the jerky motions of the figure sent chills through Kit's body. She took a step away from the figure which made its way clumsily towards her. Her eyes widened as she realised the figure that loomed towards her belonged to her father. Her body shook. She knew this was impossible. Her and Daisy had travelled back to this time, this land, this era, whereas her family was several hundred years in the future. She shook her head, stepping back as she did so.

"I know this isn't real," she shouted.

The figure gave her a toothy unearthly like grin.

"You are not real." Kit paused again. "Eva, you think you can stop us with these little tricks but I am telling you however you cannot."

She ran through her father's disfigured misty figure, she carried on through the endless dark corridors, searching for Daisy, when suddenly her arm was grabbed and pulled to the side. Her claws were fully extended and ready until she heard, "Kit, its only me!"

For a brief second, he cupped her face whilst she leant her cheek into his palm.

Chapter Thirty

Daisy was surrounded by the black, smoke-like faces swirling around her, rising from the ground, circling her, calling her name, enticing her into the darkness. Daisy could feel herself giving into these strange but somehow familiar faces.

A smoky face lunged at her then instantly disappeared. She blinked several times. She didn't quite believe what she had seen. She spun around, leaning her back against a wooden door, feeling the firm coolness pressing against her. Her heartrate increased, she heard the words: "Don't lose yourself," drifting through the rising mist.

The child-like laugh radiated around her again, her eyes widened as a small figure moved awkwardly through the mist towards her, she heard herself scream. Again, a small voice cut through the mist, "Hello, Sister, Mum and Dad wanted to say hello." Daisy stifled another scream as she looked into the dead eyes of her little sister. She felt her head spin.

Kit heard the scream, she pulled away from Destin's hand. She looked into his eyes for a second before she reached for his hand, heading through the mist towards the scream, Kit knew Eva was using dark magic but she hadn't realised how dark she had taken it. Kit had to stop this and she had to stop it now.

When suddenly she heard. "Charlie, Charlie….".

Ice-like chills ran through her, she hadn't heard that name

in years, she had almost forgotten it even existed.

She turned to see a misty face rush at her.

She sidestepped quickly whilst reciting the words, "I am not Charlie, I am not Charlie, I am not Charlie."

Destin squeezed her hand tightly. The resentment she felt towards her family rose like bile in her throat. Suddenly she felt strong hands on her shoulders shaking her. Her eyes focused on Destin's face as he suddenly embraced her in a hug, she could feel his heartrate pulsing.

She sighed into his neck. "I'm so pleased you are here, we need to find Daisy." He nodded back, taking her hand, and started to lead her through the mist.

She hadn't had anyone take control of any situations before, however, this one time she let herself be led.

Daisy felt light-headed, weary almost, as she felt herself drifting towards the faces that enticed her further into the dark mist which circled around her threateningly, surrendering herself until she felt a sudden jerk backwards. The cold steel of Kit's claws hard against her skin. She was enclosed in a warm hug.

"We need to go through the door, don't follow the faces they're just dark magic, they're not real, in fact they are just images from our past," Kit whispered in Daisy's ear. "They are memories etched into our brains which Eva is using against us," Kit finished as Daisy's body sagged against hers.

"We need to open that chamber door." She turned to Destin who had been joined by Murgo.

"You guys took some following," Murgo said, as a tiny misty claw-like hand reached out for him, he muttered more ancient protection words.

The mist evaporated before him. Destin gave the door a

quick push without it budging an inch. He motioned to Murgo to get the other side of the door. Both the men pushed, shoved and kicked at the door in vain.

Destin embedded an axe into the chamber door, the wood splintered under his effort. He carried on chopping at the door until the door gave in to Destin's axe. With a creaky groan the door opened, the group filed into the dark still chamber room, once again they had descended into darkness. Kit's eyes shone bright through the gloomy surroundings, scanning the stillness for the princess. In the furthest corner, her eyes rested on two forms, one crouching over the other.

"Eva this has gone too far." Kit's voice was steady and even.

"Not even close," Eva replied.

Kit turned to Daisy and Murgo. "I hope Bjoarn and Ethan can find the king and Queen."

Chapter Thirty-One

Bjoarn led his men through the palace front gates, up the gravel entrance, to the prestigious front doors. The stillness echoed around them. The Mage couldn't understand how quiet it was. She glanced around the empty sculpted gardens, the empty turrets and unmanned front staircase. The Mage followed Ethan as he stormed up the stone stairs through the gold and wooden door into the grand hall. Her unease growing with every step they took, yet again she glanced around the huge hallways, the high ceilings and ornate stone detailing that laced every pillar and archway. The detail that had gone into every piece of this palace took her breath away. She had never seen such splendour before.

As she gazed around in amazement, something in the corner of her eye caught her attention, a slight movement. She stopped suddenly, unease rose up into her throat, as her eyes darted around checking for any more movement. The corner was full of shadows. The Mage stared until her eyes watered, she blinked rapidly. She turned away from the corner to find the rest of the men had gone. She was all alone.

She gulped and took a deep breath, taking a step towards where she had seen the movement. She willed herself on, taking step by step until she was almost into the corner. She could feel her heart hammer inside her chest; she reached for her dagger and held it tight to her chest. The Mage stood in the darkened corner, feeling the rough stone wall, running her free hand up and down it until she hit a raised stone. She gently leant on it with a groan. The wall shifted slightly, revealing a narrow dark corridor. The Mage stifled her surprise as she peered in to the darkness, her eyes blinking several times trying to adjust to the gloom. Water ran down the wall glinting in the sliver of light that flooded the corridor. The Mage glanced back into the grand hallway, no one was there. Clutching her dagger tightly, she took a deep breath and took a step inside. The air inside the corridor felt stuffy and stagnant, it hit the back of her throat, making her cough slightly. She knew she should have gone and got Ethan, or even a torch, but she pushed herself on step by step.

The corridor became narrower the further she went into it. It became so narrow that she could feel the stones pressing against her shoulders, so she had to turn and shuffle sideways down the tunnel. Then suddenly the corridor opened out into a small rounded dark room. The air was so stagnant the Mage had to take huge gulping breaths.

"Hello, who's there?" a voice cut through the darkness.

The Mage span around, she heard the sound of fire in the corner when a face was illuminated on the other side of the room. She gasped slightly until she realised it was the king and Queen in hiding.

She took a big breath. Clutching the dagger even tighter in her hand, she took a step forward. She could see clearly the king's face, his weathered face, and his cold unblinking eyes.

"Your Majesty. it's nice to get a chance to meet you," the Mage stuttered.

The smell of burning flames fought with the stagnant air, the flame illuminated the small oppressive space which they currently occupied, casting nasty shadows which played with their eyes.

"And who may you be?" The regal voice of the king filled the space between them.

The Mage smiled slightly. "You ordered our death and you don't even know who we are." The Mage tilted her head slightly to the right with a rueful smile.

"Ahh the revolt I am assuming you're involved with," the king said, still sitting on the floor looking her up and down, noticing her moth-eaten clothing.

The Mage didn't make a move, just clutched at her dagger as so many thoughts crashed into each other inside her head.

"I saved your daughter's life," her voice was steady and clear.

The queen spoke for the first time. "Our daughter upstairs?" The anxiety and confusion laced every word.

The Mage let out a breath and shook her head. "No, the real princess. I am sorry for delivering bad news but the one in the palace who you welcomed home with open arms is an imposter, in actual fact that is Eva the lady in waiting, but in disguise."

The queen's eyes widened and her hand flew to her mouth before she could speak. "Lies," the king boomed. His voice vibrated around the tiny space.

The Mage didn't even blink.

"We have returned the real princess, the gods have saved our lives over and over again. They deserve their freedom, you have to honour that," the Mage's voice remained steady and even as she stared into the cold eyes of the king.

The king's hard stare broke into full laughter. "They serve me too well for their freedom."

The Mage's eyebrows arched at his sneering face, her eyes full of hatred. She glanced down at her dagger clutched tightly to her chest, she noticed her hands were shaking slightly as if they already knew what she was going to do.

Before her mind stopped her, she walked closer so that the light illuminated her more. The heat from the torch could be felt. She was so close she could smell his breath almost making her retch.

The blood oozed over the dagger, it spilled over the Mage's hands, for a moment she was mesmerized watching the flow of the dark red blood. The king's wide-eyed expression was full of shock. He dropped the flaming torch to the floor, casting long shadows up towards the ceiling. The Mage heard the shriek coming from the queen but she couldn't seem to tear herself away from the blood pulsing from the chest of the dying King in front of her. He convulsed slightly before slumping forward in a heap. She dragged the dagger from his chest creating a deep cavity.

"How could you?" The queen lurched at the Mage and with a quick reflex the Mage simply pushed the queen off balance.

The Mage felt like her head was under water, even in a bubble of sorts, as she heard herself say, "He was not a good man surely you realise that?"

She turned slightly unsteady on her feet, making her way back through the darkened corridor away from the heaving sobs of the queen; the king's blood covered her, dripping from her.

The bright light from the hallway startled the Mage. She brought a hand up to shield them as Ethan came rushing towards her.

He screeched to a halt as he saw the blood splattered over her, it dripped from the dagger hitting the floor with a splat.

"It's not my blood," she managed to splutter before he rushed forward, catching her before she fell to the floor.

Her world started to go black, she started to see the floor coming towards her fast as she braced herself for the impact, but it never came. As she felt the warm embrace all around her, she gave in to the feeling, closed her eyes and let the dark take her for a few seconds.

Ethan stared down at the Mage. He moved a piece of her hair from her face. He smiled softly until he heard a wail from within the wall. He glanced towards where the Mage had emerged from. He steeled himself for what may appear, however, when he saw a woman, in fact a very regal woman, she was pointing towards the Mage in his arms.

"That woman has killed the king!" she screeched in such a high volume that he winced.

Chapter Thirty-Two

"Enough!" Kit shouted whilst plunging her claws into the floor.

The stone creaked and cracked under the pressure of the claws. The ground groaned as it split and tore open.

Kit's eyes were ablaze as if a fire had been lit in them, she watched the stone floor erupt from the force of the claws digging into them. Chips of stonework flew up in the air flying everywhere, the jagged edges sharp and menacing. The ground shook, Eva stumbled forward. As she became unbalanced, she fell to her knees, losing her grip on the princess. The princess managed to roll to the left colliding with the wall with a soft thud. She tried to stand up but the pain shot through her like a wildfire.

The anger built up, welling up inside of Kit until she couldn't control it any more. A roar erupted from her mouth.

The princess looked up with shock at the noise vibrating around her, her vision blurred making her head spin as she looked at her hands as they were trying to drag her body towards the gods. Tears rolled down her face as the pain ran up and down her body. Out of the corner of her eye she saw Eva try to stumble towards her. A little shriek left her lips as she braced herself for an attack. However, after a few seconds when nothing happened, she opened her eyes to another earthquake type rumble. The princess's vision swam but she could see Kit walking with purpose towards Eva, slamming her claws into the ground causing ripple after ripple of ground shaking chaos.

Daisy, who was still stood near Murgo who was supporting her, made a move towards the princess. She grasped the wall for support as her legs kept giving way after each rumble. She felt the walls creak under the pressure that Kit was putting them under. Within seconds she had reached the princess. She ripped part of her shirt placing a firm hand over her wound and the princess squeaked in response. The blood seeped through the flimsy material.

"Murgo please help," she shouted over breathlessly, still applying firm pressure.

Eva drew her knife out, lunging at Kit clumsily; she dodged it easily and effortlessly. Eva wouldn't give up, the knife kept slashing at Kit, but with one swipe Kit knocked the knife out of Eva's hand without even blinking.

"I said enough." Kit's voice was icy and cold.

Eva launched herself at Kit, kicking, punching and thrashing away. Kit easily grabbed her wrist, holding her firmly, still Eva slumped with exhaustion breathing heavily.

"You think you have won, gods but this is nothing," she spat at Kit.

The princess rolled over, her gaze steady on Daisy and Murgo. "Where is Bjoarn?" she spoke through gritted teeth.

Murgo responded gently, "He is fighting to keep the guards at bay, your majesty."

The princess nodded her head slowly. "Have my parents been found?" she muttered, her head dropping to one side.

Daisy moved the princess so the wall supported her body and before she could answer, Ethan stumbled through the heavy chamber door carrying a blood-soaked Mage.

Daisy's mouth hung open but before she could speak Ethan stated, "It's not her blood she's okay."

"We need to get out of here," Daisy spoke firmly.

Ethan clutched the Mage firmly to his body nodding in agreement; they looked towards Kit who swiftly stabbed Eva through the heart with her claws, the claws easily sliced through her flesh, crunching through bone, cartilage and human matter. Eva screamed, blood dripping from her mouth, she tried to reach for Kit one last time.

"We shall meet again gods," she spluttered with a nasty snarl.

Eva's head slumped forward, removing her claws, Kit let the body hit the floor. She took a step back, looking at the carnage before her, she closed her eyes for a second letting her brain process what had just occurred.

"Kit, we need to leave. The princess needs medical help," Daisy muttered with urgency.

The group stumbled out of the darkened chamber; the black mist had fallen and seeped back into the underworld again leaving no trace as to what had transpired. The candles burned brightly, glowing gently, creating a warm safe glow. They walked exhaustedly through the corridors, stumbling slightly over the uneven stone slabs. Blood dripped from Kit's claws leaving a trail where she had walked. Destin walked beside her, he kept side-glancing at her, trying to read her expression but all he could see was a blank canvas. Unblinking pools of eye with no pupils. The light of the hall hit their eyes sharply making all of them wince and blink rapidly as they made their way across the vast room. Suddenly a high-pitched shriek echoed around them, a flash of white raced past them screaming, the sound vibrated around the hall. Destin grabbed the fine, flapping martial, pulling the shrieking being towards him. Within a few seconds the woman had broken free of Destin's grasp and fled into one of the many corridors. A burning sensation raced up and down him, his hand came up to his chest to find red sticky blood trickling through his shirt. He turned his head towards Kit whose eyes were filled with concern. He quickly pulled his cloak around the wound covering all trace of it. He smiled brightly at her hiding his pain.

"Mother!" the princess screamed at the fleeing figure.

The princess sagged against Murgo and Daisy. "Where is my father?" the princess whispered to Daisy.

Daisy glanced towards Ethan, who clutched the Mage to his chest. Ethan simply nodded his tired sad eyes. Daisy's eyes furrowed together. She glanced around the group as they stumbled through the hall, every one of them looked weary, almost brought to their knees with this. The effort of this battle was written across everyone's face, downcast eyes and heavy hearts.

Daisy looked back at the princess "He's dead your Majesty." Daisy's eyes were stony cold, no trace of acknowledgment, looking straight ahead.

The princess let a tear fall from her eyes resting her head. "It is for the best I suppose." she drew a deep breath.

Bjoarn placed a hand on her shoulder, looking deep into her eyes, smiling gently at her, reassurance radiating from him. She simply smiled back placing a hand on his hand.

Chapter Thirty-Three

They emerged from the palace, the clouds had parted and the sun was streaming through the broken clouds leaving a golden hue over the grounds.

"So what are we going to do now?" Daisy turned to Kit, her hand over her eyes shielding them.

The Mage blinked, her eyes open, swallowed hard speaking before Kit could form words, "The revolt will want to take over," she sighed as she spoke, letting her head hang.

"I can only speak for myself, but I will not follow the revolt, I will only follow the princess," Kit spoke with authority.

Daisy nodded her head in agreement and soon the group, one after another, kneeled in front of the princess, arms on chest in a salute.

The princess stood up, staring at the group, smiling at her new family. The princess urged the group to stand, leading the way through the palace grounds, spilling out on to the streets where the rest of the revolt and Viking men stood awaiting instruction. The princess stood before them all, her spine straight, her eyes hard, her voice steady. As she spoke clearly the towns people who had hidden behind their shuttered windows and barricaded doors began to emerge. Kit and Daisy stood either side of the princess, their claws and fangs fully extended, glinting in the sun daring anyone to question the princess's authority.

She spoke with clear crisp voice, "I am the new ruler. I am Princess Nekite. I will lead the kingdom with integrity, fairness and an open mind," her voice carried over the milling townspeople.

For a split-second, silence surrounded them until applause full of shouting and cheering erupted, even the remaining red devil warriors joined in the celebrations. The group turned back towards the palace to find the queen and start rebuilding the kingdom.

Ethan walked next to the Mage. "So, Mage, I was wondering if I could ask a question," he mumbled over his words.

The Mage arched an eyebrow at him whilst clutching at her wound. "Go on?" she kept her gaze on the floor.

"Well, the thing is I have grown rather fond of you," he stuttered again before carrying on. "I am not sure how you do this in your kingdom, but in mine it's called courting."

The Mage gave him a sideways glance. "Yes, Ethan, I would like what you call courting." She giggled slightly, holding out her hand for his.

As they walked hand in hand, she smiled to herself, running her hand through her short spiky hair, this feeling in her chest felt overwhelming as if she may burst with happiness. The last few weeks had been tough, but this was a different feeling, it made it all worthwhile.

Daisy walked behind the Mage who was holding Ethan's hand almost gleefully, skipping up the gravel driveway.

"They look happy," Murgo said with a smile.

Daisy sighed then nodded. "I'm so pleased for them, she deserves the happiness."

"What about your happiness?" Murgo asked with arched eyebrow.

"I am a god, we don't get these normal happy relationships." Daisy glanced at the floor.

"Well why not an unusual happy relationship?" Murgo laughed softly at her.

"Is that an offer?" She kept her eyes on the gravel, not daring to look him in the eyes. The breeze picked up around them, blowing her hair away from her face.

"Well, I'm a blue painted man, I'm not sure I would have what you call a normal happy relationship either so an unusual one might be just what we need." He chuckled to himself. "I was thinking of sticking around here helping out, I'm not sure how welcome I would be back in the forest, and in any case, I have liked you from the very moment I locked eyes on you." His voice calm, his eyes steady on Daisy.

Chapter Thirty-Four

Kit hung back from the group to walk with Destin, their stride falling in sync with one another.

"So what is really the plan from here on?" Destin asked through gritted teeth.

Kit cocked her head to the right, pausing for a brief moment before answering, "We need to stop the revolt, bring the princess to the throne and protect the kingdom." Kit let out a sigh whilst rubbing her eye.

"Is that what you want? You sure you don't want your peace and quiet?" He stopped abruptly, reaching for her arm.

Kit could only manage a brief shake of the head as Destin span her around.

Kit looked into Destin's eyes, his smile creasing in the corners. She lifted her hand to caress his cheek, her claws were drawn but he didn't flinch, he didn't move away, instead he leant into her hand. Kit realised she was holding her breath as her heart crashed around inside her chest. He placed his arm around her waist, drawing her in closer; she could feel his breath upon her, she took in his scent, his mouth landing on her own lips firmly. Kit closed her eyes, surrendering to the feeling of being lost in Destin's world. They pulled apart, her heart racing inside of her.

As they pulled apart, Destin folded at the waist taking in deep ragged breaths.

Kit grasped his arms, crouching down, searching his body. "What's wrong?" The panic freely flowing in her shaking voice.

He lifted his hand away from his stomach, it dripped with blood, her hand instinctively put pressure on the wound, the blood oozed around her fingers, spilled over her hand and dripped to the floor.

Kit's eyes widened as Destin fell to the floor groaning slightly as he hit the hard floor. Kit quickly knelt down facing him, a tear trickled down her face. He reached for her, holding her tightly for a second.

For that one moment she couldn't resist, she let herself be embraced. Her mind raced, the many thoughts clashed into each other but suddenly she broke away, stood, glanced around searching for a red warrior. She knew this was selfish, she knew she should let the natural action take its course, but she couldn't let him go, she wouldn't let him go, she just wouldn't watch him die.

Out of the corner of her eye she saw a wounded red warrior sneaking around the corner, she sprinted at him, sprung off her feet, giving him a sharp kick in the back. The warrior fell to his knees winded. He lay on the ground for a second, which was just enough time for Kit to grab him by the feet and drag him towards Destin.

The red warrior struggled slightly in Kit's firm grip, she felt weariness overwhelm her for a second, tears threatened to spill from her eyes. She carried on dragging the warrior where she dropped him next to Destin. Destin felt cold to the touch. She gently propped him up against the wall, shaking him to waken him. He groaned slightly, keeping hold of his wounded stomach.

Puzat stood guard watching over them as Kit plunged her claws into the warrior, drawing out his heart she placed it on the ground, etching a circle around them all. Kit held Destin in her arms, staring deep into his eyes her world swam as tears freely flowed from her eyes. She began reciting the ancient words. The ground shook, ancient faces rose from the ground in a blue mist swirling around the circle gathering momentum.

Her sobs became so great she could barely speak, she choked on her words as she watched the life drain from Destin.

The ground stopped shaking, the mist seeped back into the earth, the faces that occupied the mist crawled back into the underworld. Once again, the world was quiet. Kit stared into the lifeless body that belonged to Destin, another tear hit his forehead, then suddenly his eyes sprang open. The bright blue coloured eyes stared back into her own.

Printed in Great Britain
by Amazon